I0545323

The Wendigo Witchling

The Skinwalkers' Witchling Trilogy

Book 2

B. Kristin McMichael

The Wendigo Witchling
Copyright © 2016 by B. Kristin McMichael
www.bkristinmcmichael.com
All rights reserved.

Lexia Press, LLC
P.O. Box 982
Worthington, OH 43085
www.lexiapress.com

ISBN-10: 1-941745-83-0
ISBN-13: 978-1-941745-83-0

Cover design: Jessica Allain
Editor: Kathie Middlemiss of Kat's Eye Editing
Melissa of There For You Editing
Proofing: Ashton M. Brammer

This book is licensed for your personal use only. No part of this
book may be reproduced in any form or by electronic or
mechanical means without written permission of the author. All
names, characters, and places are fiction and any resemblance to
real, living or dead, is entirely coincidental.

CONTENTS

CHAPTER 1

Cassandra Booth didn't look back as she ran. She was getting better at dodging people on the street. Turning the corner, she dashed into the town's only used clothing store. There were a few straggling shoppers who were scouring the racks for deals, but that didn't matter to her. Cassie ran to the back of the store and the changing rooms, grabbing a bottle of perfume on the way.

It was only the fourth time in the last twenty-four hours she had tried to run away. She may have bonded herself to school heartthrob Nathaniel Bay, but that didn't mean she was planning on anything changing. She did it to save her friend. She had no intention of getting married at sixteen to a guy she hadn't spoken to in years before he was suddenly chosen as her mate. The night human world was nuts, and she wanted out.

"You need to pay for that," the cashier told her.

Cassie waved at the middle-aged lady before ducking under the curtain which led to the back rooms.

She ran past the first few rooms before stepping into the third one. Quickly she touched everything in the room with her bare hand. Stepping back into the hallway, she doused herself with the cheap perfume. She didn't need to be a night human to smell how obnoxious the stuff was. Cassie hurried down the hallway and placed the empty bottle on the counter in the last room, along with the only money she had with her. She didn't care how much the stuff cost. Cassie had left more than it was worth as she snuck out the employee back door into an empty hallway.

Cassie slid down behind the door and waited, hoping to be rid of the smell as soon as she could get away.

Her life was getting more and more complicated since the ceremony to make her part of the coven drew closer. It wasn't just a bonding ceremony they were planning; they wanted to drain all of her witch powers. Cassie didn't plan to stick around for that. No way was she just going to sit around and hope they changed their minds. Nate had planned how to get her out of it. Or so he said. Where was he now? He had been missing in action for four days straight. Cassie knew the coven wanted her and her powers, and she wasn't about to do as they wished. She had to get away, and she needed to leave now.

"She backtracked again," one male voice said on the other side of the door.

"Any trail?" another person replied.

"No. She's getting better at this. Check back in the store; we must have missed it," the first voice responded.

"Well, I'm not going to be any use now with that smell. I'll be lucky if I can find her in a week. You should have never told her how much you hate perfume," the second grumbled.

Cassie smiled. She couldn't care less if Nic Welch was going to lose his sense of smell for a week. That was his own fault for telling her about his great dislike of perfume. She didn't know if all skinwalkers were that sensitive, but it seemed likely.

"Mikel is going to kill us for losing her again," Nic told the other guy. He kicked in the door of the last changing room. Cassie held her breath, hoping he wouldn't suspect the empty perfume bottle was hers.

"Only if we don't come back with her, and I, for one, am not going to give up looking until I find her," the first replied. They didn't even come to the back door that read "Employees Only".

Cassie continued to hold her breath as they walked away. This was the furthest she had gotten away from the night humans keeping her captive. Well, she wasn't exactly being held in one place; they just never let her be alone, even in her own room at home. The first few days she didn't noticed the people following her, but once Nate went missing, she began to see people around her more. Someone even sat outside her house, watching her bedroom window at night. Creepy. It was her best friend, Whitney, who spilled the beans and was now forbidden from seeing her. Once Cassie realized what was going on, she tried to get away. That was her first mistake—thinking she could get away. Saying Nate was upset was an understatement. He had put her on lockdown, and only had just allowed her to leave her house since her first attempt to run away. They were holding her captive in her own home, and her uncle went right along with it.

Now she just needed to make it to some sort of vehicle if she wanted to get away. She hadn't thought it through that much. It was more of a spur of the moment decision this time. Planning gave them an edge to stop her.

'Cassie, just go back to them,' Nate pleaded over the bond and the direct line into Cassie's head with his voice.

He had been physically gone, but somehow seemed to know what she was up to all the time. She needed help understanding night humans, and Whitney had told her enough to know what to do. There was a small town she needed to go to visit in the mountains that filled with night humans. Maybe they would have answers.

She had traveled across the country the summer before to help out a friend. While there, she had broken a blood bond, even though it was only temporary. Given enough time, maybe she could break her unwanted bond with Nate. At the very least, she could learn more about night humans and what it meant to be bonded to one.

'I told you that I was only doing the spell to save

Whitney. I don't want to be bonded to you,' Cassie replied to Nate.

It had been easier than she thought, talking to him over the bond they shared, and quicker than a cell phone. The only problem was she couldn't hang up on him.

'Doesn't matter. Mating bonds are for life,' Nate answered. *'Now go back to them before you get yourself in trouble.'*

'Life? Well, we'll see about that.'

'Don't make me come find you,' Nate threatened.

Cassie looked out the exit door. Someone was bringing packages to donate to the store and had left their car running. She was pretty sure stealing a car was a crime, probably even a felony, but what other options did she have? Cassie stepped out of the building and smiled at the blond-haired girl leaning against the wall. Whitney gave her a big smile in return.

'Cassie, get your butt home. John and Maria are going to be upset.' Nate sounded so parental Cassie had to try not to laugh since he was only just over a year older than her.

'Good for them. Maybe they'll think twice about keeping everything from me.'

'Cassie.' Nate was no longer teasing. He sounded very angry.

'Good luck finding me.'

She slid into the passenger seat as Whitney got in the driver's side.

"Where to, bestie?" Whitney asked, pulling back her long blond hair into a ponytail.

"Triclan City." *The* place for night humans. If anyone could help her, she would be able to find them there. Cassie needed answers, and she needed them soon before she got too caught up in the night human world to be able to get out. It was time for a road trip.

Cassie didn't realize the drive would be as long as it was. It wasn't like she had been on a road trip before in her entire life. The only trips she took were on flights with her aunt to the only place in the U.S. that had other witches. Her uncle had finally explained to her that he couldn't leave town without major negotiations between various night humans because of how all the different kinds were very territorial. If he stepped into the wrong place, it could mean serious repercussions or even death if he ran across enemies. Cassie felt lucky that she was only bonded to a night human. As a day human, she could still go wherever she pleased.

She looked at her friend as she drove. Whitney didn't seem to have a care in the world. Cassie was a day human, but her friend was not.

"Won't you get in trouble for leaving?" she asked.

Whitney shrugged. "They've kept you locked up for days. I don't care what sort of trouble I get into if it means you get a break from all the crazy."

"Aww," Cassie replied.

"Besties forever." Whitney held up a fist for Cassie to bump, and she did so.

Reaching down, Whitney began to scroll through radio channels since the last one was going out of range. It was the third time since they began their trip that they needed to change stations.

"I told my mom that not getting the upgrade would suck. Guess she didn't plan on any road trips." Whitney kept scrolling, not finding much to listen to.

"Because you guys can't travel without getting into trouble, right?" Cassie asked.

Whitney was a night human along with her brother and father. Cassie was beginning to get nervous the further away they drove. She wasn't exactly sure what the rules were that would keep her night human friend safe.

"My dad can't travel, and I don't think my mother wanted to go anywhere fun without him. It would make him sad to miss out."

"But you can travel through different night human territories?" It was all very new to Cassie. She had only learned, less than two weeks ago, that night humans who lived off human blood actually existed. She was still trying to understand everything, but nothing made much sense.

"If I keep to the main road, then it isn't a problem. We can't take any shortcuts or anything," Whitney explained. "And because I'm not a full member of the pack, other night humans don't see me as a threat, at least not yet."

Cassie nodded. That made sense... she hoped. She wanted out and away from Nate and the clan that wouldn't leave her alone, but she didn't want Whitney in danger because of it. The lull of the car as Whitney drove was soothing after being on edge for so many days. Cassie had no clue why Nate was gone so much, but it seemed like something was going on around her. And the constant guard kept her suspicious of every sound. Leaning back, Cassie closed her eyes. She was safe with Whitney, and finally able to relax.

'Where are you going?' Nate asked. He was more concerned than mad now. His moods seemed to fluctuate like the weather.

'Away,' Cassie replied. She wanted to add *from you*, but by this point, it was from everyone. Cassie felt the slight pressure of voices as they faded from her mind, like a whisper that she couldn't make out the words from.

"Man, is he mad this time," Whitney commented as she continued to drive.

"Who's mad?" Cassie asked. Opening her eyes, she looked at her friend.

Whitney flipped her blond curls over her shoulder and drove with one hand, completely ignoring the cars around her. If it had been Cassie's first time in the car, she would have been scared, but after months of riding with Whitney, she knew that her friend had a sixth sense for keeping the car on the road and accident-free.

"Than," Whitney replied with Nate's much *cooler* name. Well, at least according to everyone at school once he began to go by it.

Cassie shrugged. He was mad, but it was to be expected. He didn't seem to understand anyone not doing exactly as he told them. He had been that way since he was a kid. Cassie used to think it was funny; now he seemed like more of a spoiled brat than anything.

"He just won't stop screaming at me," Whitney added.

Cassie scrunched up her eyes and peered closely at her friend. Her phone was still on the emergency brake between them. *How's Nate yelling at Whitney?*

"In my head," Whitney added, sensing her friend's confusion.

"Your head?" Cassie had thought it was strange enough when she first heard Nate's voice in her head after they bonded, but now it didn't seem like it was strange at all.

"We are a pack," Whitney explained. "We can communicate without words like your mating allows you, because we spend half our time in a form that doesn't use words. And it isn't like we're all the same animal. We have to be able to communicate like this."

"Since you hear his voice, do you hear mine, too?" Cassie asked. She thought of the word *banana* to see if it would work.

Whitney laughed.

"No, but Than just heard that and told me to tell you to stop blocking him out," Whitney added.

"Blocking him out? Does he really think I have a clue what I'm doing? I mean, you just told me that you can hear him, which is news to me. I have no clue about any of this. No one would answer my questions when they held me hostage." Cassie crossed her arms in front of her chest. It was annoying to always be in the dark about everything, but even more now that she was supposed to be part of the *in-*

crowd. She still didn't know anything, but everyone expected her to.

Whitney smiled. "That's precisely why we need to get away. They're treating you like a child one minute and then like an adult the next, and expecting you to know everything. Really? They suck. We need some time for you to see the night human world without all the crappy parts of being mated to someone without a choice."

Cassie nodded. That was exactly what she was thinking. The only difference was that now she wasn't just mated like Whitney thought, but actually bonded to Nate. It was a lot more serious and permanent. She hadn't meant to bond to him, but it was kind of her fault for choosing to make the protection potion with her own blood. He was right; she could have lied and acted perplexed when it didn't work on the silver, but she'd been too worried about saving Whitney.

'Cassie, please come back,' Nate pleaded across the bond. *'I know this is all new. I can help you.'*

'No. I need some time away from this, and I'll come back once I'm ready.' Cassie really couldn't stay away forever like she wanted to do. It would be much easier to run away than face the fact that she was now essentially married to Nate, and they were only sixteen.

'Then I'll be waiting,' Nate replied, shocking Cassie. She hadn't expected that.

'Really?'

'Really. I know I've been busy, but I've wanted to be with you every minute. I know you're scared and frustrated by all this. I get that. I'm just trying to make it easier, but it will take some time. The coven still thinks we need to bond, and they're making plans to take your power during the bonding. Your aunt did an excellent spell to cover up the bond, but I have to tread softly to keep them from finding out, and I need everything to fall into place before the ceremony. That's why I've been gone. I really would rather be with you and help you learn about all of this.' Nate sounded sincere. Cassie

almost wanted to give in and go back to him. Whitney kept driving.

'I need to get away from all this.' Cassie held firm though it was hard. Part of her had just forgiven him for everything in the past week. She hated when Nate acted like the friend she had grown up with and not the annoying Than that he was now most of the time.

'I get that. Just please stay safe. Don't leave Whitney's side. She'll take care of you,' Nate told her. He had complete faith in Whitney, even if he was still a bit mad under the surface.

More whispering filled Cassie's head. She shook it to try to make it dim down. She hated how it had been happening more often. She almost felt like she was losing her mind. It had to do with the bond, but it was just yet another thing she knew very little about.

Whitney kept driving, still trying to find a radio station. Nate's presence in Cassie's mind grew fainter along with the other voices.

"We'll be out of his range soon," Whitney told Cassie. "Any last words you'd like me to tell Lover Boy?"

Cassie rolled her eyes. "Lover Boy? Really?"

"Well, I figured Eye Candy could be offensive since he's your mate. Mates normally get mad, even if someone is just speaking about their bond-partner that way."

"Nope, no anger here. In fact, I'm more than happy to get away, and you can call him anything you want to," Cassie replied.

The thread connecting Cassie to Nate mentally grew even quieter, and so did all the voices.

"I won't miss that part."

"What part?" Whitney asked.

"All those voices in my head. It was getting a little full," Cassie complained. Taking a deep breath, she enjoyed the mental silence.

"Voices?"

"Yeah, whenever Nate and I talked in my head, there were always more voices," Cassie explained.

Whitney swerved, barely missing the car she was passing on the narrow, two-lane road. "You didn't," she said, accusing Cassie.

Cassie's eyes widened. She had no clue what Whitney was talking about... again. The night human world was too complicated to keep up with as it was, and then to add Whitney and her enthusiasm on top of it, Cassie was genuinely confused.

"Didn't ..."

"You bonded to him," Whitney accused with a big grin on her face. "You actually bonded to him."

Cassie quickly put her hands over her friend's mouth.

"Don't say that out loud. I wasn't supposed to tell anyone."

Whitney wiggled her eyebrows, but Cassie didn't move her hands. Whitney waited, and Cassie finally relented as it was close to impossible to hold her friend's mouth shut with her seatbelt on.

"I'm not anyone. I'm your best friend, and man we have much more to talk about now." Whitney grinned as she passed yet another car. "My best friend went and grew up without telling me. She bonded herself to a night human. That's something you don't forget to tell your friend, and I'm sorry, the no tell policy doesn't hold for best friends. This is one life milestone you don't get to keep to yourself. Once we get to our hotel, you have to tell me every detail. *Every detail.*"

Cassie shook her head. There weren't many details, especially not the ones Whitney wanted. At least Cassie got the basics of a night human bond; it had to deal with love and wanting to be connected forever. Most of the time the bond formed between people who were mates and essentially married. Whitney did tell her that people who were friends could also bond, but Cassie knew what Whitney was thinking, and it was far from the truth.

Even though she was bonded, she needed to get out of it. It had been done to save her friend, and that was all. Her feelings for Nate—which were still growing—had nothing to do with it. And the night human Jared, who tried to explain more about the bond to her, had to be wrong. He claimed you couldn't get bonded unless you wanted to be. Cassie didn't choose to be Nate's mate, and she sure didn't want to be bonded to him. Yet it had still worked. You could bond someone you didn't want to be with. She was living proof of that. At least, she needed to keep telling herself that.

CHAPTER 2

Cassie **waited behind** her friend in line. She had no clue what they were doing or what was going on, but she kept her mouth shut. Whitney had said to let her do all the talking, and Cassie was following her instructions. They had parked the car almost an hour ago and had been waiting in the line since. Whitney didn't talk as they stood there, and neither did Cassie. She didn't know what was going on, but Whitney seemed a bit on edge. As Whitney finally approached the counter, Cassie followed close behind. Moving over, Whitney let Cassie stand beside her.

"Name, kind," the teenage boy at the counter squeaked out.

Cassie guessed he was even younger than they were from his size and voice.

"Whitney Mallory of the skinwalker clan," Whitney replied. The boy turned to Cassie. She looked blankly at the guy. Whitney answered for her, "Cassandra Booth, day human of skinwalker descent."

The boy nodded, and then held out a computerized contraption with a hole in it. Whitney placed her hand in the hole with a picture of a palm faced up on it. The handheld computer thing beeped, and a light turned on and ran a light over the hand. The boy took a second one from behind the counter and held it out to Cassie. She placed her hand inside just as her friend had. The light turned on, and she felt the sides of the box press tighter to her hand. Suddenly there was a sharp pinch to her pinky finger.

"Ouch," Cassie complained as she tried to pull her hand

from the box.

The guy looked at Cassie like she was the strange one, but didn't let go of the box. The light stopped moving, and the box let go of Cassie's hand. She pulled it out immediately.

The boy glanced down. "Entry denied," he read out on the machine.

"Denied?" Cassie asked in disbelief.

"You're not just a day human," the boy replied, pointing to the scanner which had just tried to eat Cassie's hand. "Anyone who is part of a ruling family must seek permission to visit before coming so that the proper welcome can be made."

"I'm not part of any ruling family," Cassie replied. *What is he talking about?*

"Ugh," Whitney groaned. "You're Than's mate and thus part of the ruling family. I didn't think about that. I figured your family or mine had called ahead of us and wanted us home. They didn't, but this ..." Whitney shook her head like she should have guessed as much.

Cassie groaned, too. Their road trip was being cut short. She just wanted to get away, and now that was being foiled by Nate, and he wasn't even there.

"Well, technically, she isn't part of the family yet. She has yet to complete all the bonding rituals and right now is still under her own family," Whitney added, batting her eyes and using her movie star looks to try to win over the guy.

"Completely true," Cassie added, trying her best to imitate her friend and her "pretty please" face.

The guy glanced first at Cassie, and then at Whitney. He gave in. "I need to verify this with my boss," he said before he turned and walked away.

"This is ridiculous. That thing bit me," Cassie complained in a hushed voice.

Whitney grinned. "Um, that's what it was supposed to do. It had to test your blood to make sure you're telling the truth about who you are."

"You could have warned me," Cassie complained.

Whitney gave her an evil grin. "What would be the fun in that?"

Cassie hit her friend's arm. She hadn't noticed, but all around them people at the counter were doing exactly what they had done. Several of them appeared as shocked as Cassie when they were pricked.

"Day humans," Whitney explained. "Night humans don't feel pain the same way as day humans. A prick in the finger is nothing compared to being turned into our night forms."

Cassie nodded, and two new people moved to the front of the line next to them. Each one took a turn putting their hand in the machine. Neither one flinched. Night humans- but what kind exactly? Cassie had been told the basics, such as that there were over twenty different kinds of night humans that held territories in the US alone, but she didn't know much more beyond that. Cassie looked around the room, scanning for where their guy had gone. He was busy talking to an older lady. The boy was being talked to quite strictly before she noticed the large... well, extremely large picture behind the two of them. There was an enormous red-bearded man standing with his petite, blond-haired wife along with two grown sons. The one on the right was almost as big as the father and looked like he would have a beard in no time, but it was the one on his left that caught Cassie's attention. The reddish-brown-haired boy was only a few years older than them, and Cassie had met him once before.

"Why is Turner's picture on the wall and that big?" Cassie asked Whitney as the young man who took their palm scans and blood returned with his boss.

"He's the second son of the leader here," Whitney replied. "Wait a second. How do you know who he is? You've never met any other night humans."

"I met him this summer. He's one of Devin's friends." Peering closer at the picture, she decided it had to be at least a couple years old. "And he has his left ear pierced now. I can't decide which way looks better."

The older blonde looked at Cassie, assessing her. "Are you saying you know Turner Winter?" she asked in disbelief.

"I guess," Cassie replied, still unsure what it meant.

Reaching down, the lady picked up the phone at the station with a smug look on her face. She dialed a number while they watched, still not being told a thing. Whitney held her breath, as hopeful as Cassie that some good luck would fall on them. They both needed a break from their current lives.

"Yes, please connect me through to Master Turner's butler," she said to the person on the other end of the line and looked at Cassie like she was in trouble.

"Butler?" Cassie whispered. *Who had a butler?*

Whitney grinned and quickly covered Cassie's mouth. *Ooops.* She was supposed to let Whitney do all the talking.

"Has Master Turner been with Lord Devin this summer?" she asked, checking on Cassie's story.

At first, Cassie wanted to ask why that even mattered, but she bit her tongue instead. *Master. Lord. What sort of world are we in?* Cassie just knew them as Turner and Devin. The lady made them sound like these very important people, not a family friend who asked them to stop by to break a spell and then fight hand-to-hand with two witches. Cassie didn't know anything about lords and masters, but the title alone made it seem like they didn't do things that taxing.

"And did he spend time with a Cassandra Booth, mate to the heir to the Skinwalker clan?" she asked the person.

"Cassie and Maria," Whitney added. No one called Cassie Cassandra.

"Cassie and Maria," the lady corrected, tapping her foot impatiently. The voice on the other end abruptly stopped, and Cassie quickly recognized the voice that was now chewing out the lady. Her smug expression disappeared immediately. "I'm very sorry. I'll let her and her friend pass immediately."

Whitney smiled nicely at the young man as he pulled out two cards to hand them over to them.

"Master Turner said to tell you he will pick you up from the hotel for dinner tonight, but to have a fun time exploring until then," the lady explained, bowing her head to Cassie. "I'm sorry to have been an inconvenience for you, Lady Bay."

Cassie opened her mouth to correct her for using Nate's last name instead of her own, but Whitney clamped her hand down. Then, she took the two cards which had been printed for them by the younger guy. Whitney grinned, and before anyone else could stop them, hurried to the door off to the left side of the room, away from the larger-than-life-sized picture of Turner.

"You didn't tell me you met Turner this summer," Whitney exclaimed as they headed out the door to the waiting cabs. Whitney flashed the cab driver the new IDs they had just received, and he even bowed to Cassie. Cassie was ready to do an Aunt Maria rant on her friend, but Whitney shook her head.

"Would you ladies like to go to the hotel or downtown first?" the older man asked, keeping his eyes from meeting Cassie's.

"Hotel first," Whitney decided for them.

Cassie opened her mouth to speak, and Whitney quickly put her hand over it again to keep her from saying something. Keeping quiet—especially with Whitney—was a hard if not impossible task. She had too many questions and a few objections, but Whitney was doing what was best for them. Her questions would have to wait.

The cabbie drove through a tunnel leading into town, and Cassie watched out the window. The parking garage and entry into town were farther back than she realized. She thought town was just on the other side of the tunnel. The cabbie whizzed through the dark before coming to the other side. Cassie could see a whole big city sprawled out before them. The car continued to whip down the road into town, and he only slowed once they reached the first houses. Cassie was glad he did. It gave her a chance to look around at the night human world, which was just waking for their day. She tried to keep her mouth from dropping as people passed by that looked just about as scary as the creatures that hunted her the week before. Seeing her reaction, Whitney laughed.

"This is why we needed to come here. You have to see the real night human world and not that house they have you locked away in." Whitney grinned.

"No wonder Nate told me to remain with you to stay safe," Cassie replied as they passed a creature that was twice as big as any man she had ever seen, and paler than someone who hadn't been out in the sun for years.

Whitney laughed again. "They aren't dangerous. Everyone here has to go through the same way we came and be let in. They're all here peacefully. Than's just overprotective."

Cassie wanted to think that, but as they passed a man who was more snake than human, she didn't think he was way too out of line. So many of the people walking around were odd enough to haunt her dreams for life, and knowing that they fed on day human blood made her realize she wasn't going anywhere in the city without her best friend.

"Here's the Santiago Hotel," the cabbie stated as he pulled the car to a stop in front of a three-story, white-walled, glamorously decorated building.

He hurried out of the car faster than humanly possible to get Cassie's door before she could open it. *Night human*, she thought. At least, he wasn't scary-looking. The cabbie waited with the open door, still bowing his head to her.

"Um, thanks," Cassie said as she slid out with Whitney right behind her.

"My pleasure, Lady Bay," the man replied.

Cassie was going to object again, but Whitney grabbed her arm and pulled her through the open doors of the enormous hotel. Cassie glanced at her friend, but she ignored her pleading look. They were far from alone, and she had a feeling Whitney didn't want everyone to know how new Cassie was to the world. She acted like it was safe, but Cassie had a clue that strolling around without knowledge of the place wasn't exactly safe.

Walking to the desk, Whitney held their cards out to the person who was behind it and talking on the phone. As soon as she saw Cassie's card, she hung up without saying good-bye.

"Welcome to the Santiago Hotel," she greeted with a slight accent. "How many nights can we have the pleasure of your company?"

"We will be here until Sunday," Whitney answered.

"But the coven is on Friday night," Cassie told her friend. Whitney wasn't part of the coven, but her mother was, so Cassie assumed her mother told her about it.

Whitney grinned wickedly. "That's why we'll be here until Sunday." Yep. Whitney already knew.

The girl behind the counter began to type in the details before pausing to scan the cards, then continued to type.

"Will the president's suite do for your visit?" she asked.

"That would be great," Whitney replied with her thousand-watt smile. She was a complete natural at it.

"How the heck—" Cassie got out before Whitney stepped on her foot to distract her. "Ow." She looked up at her friend.

With her back to the receptionist, Whitney mouthed the words, 'Please stay quiet.'

"We've given you the suite on the top floor. It comes fully stocked, but should you need anything else just let us know," the girl added, handing Whitney their cards back. Smiling, Whitney nodded. "I can get someone to take your bags to your room," she offered.

"We traveled light since it's only the weekend. I'll take care of it." Whitney hefted the mostly-empty bag for the receptionist to see.

"Great. Elevators to three and the only door on the left," she explained before bowing to Cassie.

Cassie stared at the top of the head of the girl. Everything made less sense since they arrived. What was with all the bowing to her? Whitney looped her arm in Cassie's and dragged her to the elevator.

As soon as the door closed, Cassie turned to her friend.

"You have a lot of explaining to do. What the heck is going on?" Cassie put her hands on her hips as she stared at her friend.

"I'm not completely sure, but it seems your mating bond registers on their little blood meters. Since you're bonded to Than, our next alpha, that basically makes you a princess in the night human world. This is great. We're going to have so much fun here, even more than I had planned. It's like a free ticket to do anything," Whitney gushed.

"And how do we pay for this? I'm pretty sure your parents will see that on your credit card when we leave."

They had gotten in more than a little trouble the year before when Whitney decided her emergency credit card from her parents should be used for a night on the town when she was depressed after failing her witchling class at school. There wasn't much to do in their town, but they had managed between the mall, Guiro's Italian restaurant, and the private chauffeur Whitney rented to charge more than Cassie was sure her uncle made in a month.

"That's the best part. You're royalty now. You don't have to pay for a thing. This is all given to you," Whitney replied. "I honestly didn't think this would happen this soon. I figured people would have to be able to see your bond, but those magic machines made it happen. This is great. This will be great. You will forget all about your crappy week."

The elevator bell dinged as they stopped on their floor. Whitney made a grand bow to Cassie, who clunked her on the head in response.

"This way, my liege," Whitney said in her best British accent.

At that, Cassie rolled her eyes and went to the left in the direction the receptionist had pointed her. She stopped at the door. They hadn't been given any key to open it.

Whitney reached past Cassie and swiped the ID card she was holding.

"This baby gets you everything around here," she explained, pushing open the door.

Cassie paused at the doorway. When they reached the mountains on their drive, Nate and all the voices with him disappeared. She hadn't heard or felt him since, but something now nagged at her. Something felt out of place. Cassie peered into the lavish room in front of her. It was strange and almost like a fairy tale. Whitney was grinning as she opened the balcony door. She was more than relaxed; she was ecstatic. Cassie had to be worrying about nothing. What could go wrong? They were going to get to play princesses for a weekend.

Cassie glanced down at her dirty jeans and T-shirt. If Whitney was right, and Turner was some sort of royalty amongst the night humans, then was it really appropriate to meet him in the clothing she just ran away in half a day ago?

"We will go shopping later," Whitney told her as she pulled her to the elevator. Turner had called and was already downstairs waiting for them.

"Yeah, but he's royalty here," Cassie complained.

He hadn't said he was the last time she met him, and she would have never guessed, but everything now was very clear, from the portrait on the wall in the entrance to their pictures on everything official in the hotel room. Turner was a prince in the night human world they were now in.

"And so are you, don't worry," Whitney replied.

Cassie highly doubted it, even if her pass said it bold and clear. She didn't want to even look at it because it didn't say Cassie Booth but rather Cassandra Bay, mate to Nathaniel Bay. It made her cringe just to see her name as if she were already married. She might not have liked her last name much as it was, but it was still hers, and now it was gone.

The elevator ride down was quick, and the door dinged as it opened. Locking her arm in Cassie's, Whitney pulled her out into the hallway and to the lobby. She knew all too well that if left to her own, Cassie would have stayed on the elevator to go back to their room.

"I promise we won't stay out too late," Whitney told her as they turned the corner to get a full view of the lobby.

"We better not. Do you know this is the first time in almost a week I don't have all those extra voices in my head? I'll finally be able to sleep," Cassie complained.

"You know, if you weren't here and were in the outside day human world, a comment like that would most likely get you locked away in a psych ward," a male voice said from behind them.

Whitney spun them both around to the person talking. He grinned at them with his boyish charm and reddish brown hair. He was just as handsome as the last time Cassie saw him. She was beginning to think that being a night human made you look better. It was strange that everyone around her was good-looking growing up, but now she could see it was because they were all night humans.

"Glad to see someone let you in on our little secret," Turner continued. "And who may you be?"

"Little?" Cassie mumbled as Turner took Whitney's hand and kissed it.

Whitney blushed.

"This is my friend, Whitney," Cassie added, as they stared at each other.

"Mm-hmm." Turner nodded to Whitney. "A cat. I like

kitties."

Whitney blushed further and was a loss for words. Cassie couldn't help but stare at her friend. Whitney was never a loss for words.

"What brings you guys to town?" Turner asked as he offered an arm to both Whitney and Cassie at the same time.

"Well, she accidently got a mate, and we were able to tell her everything, but they decided to lock her away. I had to orchestrate a prison break. This was the only place I could think of where we would both be welcome; I figured Cassie needed to go on a good, old-fashioned road trip," Whitney explained as she finally came back to her senses. She took his arm, and he led them out of the hotel lobby and onto the sidewalk. Turner led them on their walk, taking them further into the downtown.

"And we didn't know it was going to cause a problem," Cassie added.

Turner laughed. "I have a feeling anywhere you go will cause a problem," Turner replied. "I've met the Bay family before, and they are very possessive. How in the world did you get mated to a night human without knowing about them?"

"Guess you don't have to know the truth to form a bond. It can be all on secrets and lies," Cassie said a bit more bitterly than she had intended.

Turner didn't miss a beat as he laughed more. "You're one of the strangest day humans I've ever met." He stopped at an ice cream store.

"I'd rank you in my list of night humans, but I'm not too sure who I've met that was one or not," Cassie replied. "It's still all so confusing. Whitney said the sidhe are night humans, but I never once saw anyone drink blood while I was there."

"Devin, nope; Nessa, yes," Turner explained, naming two people Cassie had met.

"Which makes even less sense," Cassie complained,

Whitney stepped forward to look at the selection of ice cream. "Devin was casting sidhe magic left and right. How is he not one?" Cassie wanted a handbook to explain it all.

"Devin's a special case." Turner looked at the worker.

"What can I get you?" the teen behind the counter asked, finally finding a spot to speak.

Whitney grinned like a child in a candy shop. "Strawberry cheesecake."

"Chocolate truffle," Turner ordered.

Cassie looked at the case. They were discussing night humans that drank blood while standing in what seemed like a normal ice cream store. It was very surreal. If she hadn't met the night humans and seen the monsters who tried to kill her with her own eyes, she would have never believed anyone.

"Mint chip for her," Whitney ordered for Cassie when she didn't speak.

In the blink of an eye, all three cones were in front of them. Whitney reached up and took hers without hesitation while Turner grabbed both his and Cassie's. Cassie just stood and stared at the person behind the counter. He looked like a normal teen boy. He had scraggly brown hair, which needed to be cut, and a pierced eyebrow that made you look at his sky blue eyes. But what he didn't have was long pointed fangs, nor did he just use magic. She would have sensed it. Nope. The clank of the ice cream scooper as it sloshed around in the water behind the counter was enough to know that he scooped them, just faster than Cassie could see.

Turner led the way back outside to a table that was alone on one side of the doorway. He pulled out a chair for Whitney, who gave him a blond hair toss before sitting down and batting her eyes at him. Cassie didn't wait for him as she pulled out her own chair and sat down next to her friend.

At that, Turner chuckled. He seemed to find Cassie amusing, and she found Turner about as serious as the last time she met him. They had been hunting for a rogue witch in the sidhe village, and he was smiling the whole time. Even when he was fake-pouting at something or another that Devin had said, he was still smiling.

"I get the feeling your welcome to the night human world didn't go as well as your aunt hoped it would?" Turner raised an eyebrow. He had met her aunt last summer, too.

"Welcome? I wouldn't call it that," Cassie replied.

Nothing thus far had even come close to welcoming. She still had too much to learn, and the coven planned to strip her of her powers in just days. Even if Nate told her he was going to save her from that, what could one night human do against the coven? They held the power.

"Let's see. She got a mate, not of her choosing, almost was killed by a wendigo, was locked in her house for a day, met family she wasn't supposed to meet, and found out that her options pretty much suck. Yeah, I'd say that didn't go as anyone planned," Whitney stated, giving the CliffsNotes version of Cassie's new life.

"Oh, and you forgot the latest house arrest I'm doing right now," Cassie added. "Of which I'm in your debt for finding me and breaking me out before I ended up stabbing one of those annoying *friend*s of Nate who wouldn't let me even pee in peace and quiet. Nic actually followed me to the bathroom yesterday and told me that he had to watch guard over me. As I peed."

Turner's grin went from a smile to laughter at Cassie's comment. She couldn't help but chuckle with him; his laughter was just too contagious.

"Let me get this straight; you've been put under house arrest twice now?" Turner asked.

"In one week," Whitney added with a grin. She was laughing alongside them.

Turner let out another laugh. "Devin isn't going to believe me when I tell him this." Turner wiped his eyes from laughing too hard. "If I hadn't met you before, I would swear you had to be my little sister from some alternative universe. Twice in one week. You make me very proud."

"Then the rumors about you are true?" Whitney asked, her eyes sparkling as she thought.

"Rumors?" Cassie asked, looking between them.

"Let's just say he isn't the heir to his clan, and there are more reasons than just that he's the second son," Whitney replied cryptically. "And that his father claims every white hair on his head came from Turner."

Again Turner gave a boisterous laugh, causing passersby to look in their direction. When they noticed it was Turner, they nodded and kept walking.

"Some might say that I'm a bit rebellious. Ahh, I'd say I just like to do things my way. Why worry what other people think or want? It's my life to live," Turner explained. "Now, my father doesn't exactly view life the same way, and neither does my older brother, but oh well. They're the ones bogged down by duty. Not me."

Cassie could only wish she could be that brave. Her whole life was filled with people running it for her. Her uncle decided what she could do, when she could go places, and to some extent even what she could wear or what he was willing to buy her. This road trip was the first time in her life someone else wasn't telling her what to do. Well, Whitney had been telling her what to do a bit, but that didn't count. That was just Whitney.

"I'm guessing from the little you've told me that I should inform my father you're not up to a formal welcome and would like this trip to be incognito," Turner suggested.

"Formal welcome?" Cassie squeaked out.

Turner grinned at her response.

"Yep, no welcome. And if you could keep this from the clan for the most part, that would be great. As soon as they can they'll be coming for us anyway," Whitney replied. "We'd like to have as much fun as we can now, because who knows how long before they'll let Cassie out of their sight again. In fact, Than might just chain himself to her to keep her in one place after this trip."

"You're teasing, right?" Cassie asked quickly.

"About not getting freedom ever again in your life? No, not in the least. I was excited we got it to work as well as we did to get away. Than won't let that happen again," Whitney replied. "He's probably freaking out right now."

Cassie stared at her friend. Whitney didn't seem to care in the least, but Cassie knew better. Nate wasn't the freaking out kind. He was more the *plot and get revenge* kind. And that didn't bode well for Cassie, or Whitney for that matter. Yes, incognito would be the best.

"Well, in that case, let me be your personal guide to the city. If there's anything you want to see or do, I can make it happen. And we don't need anything formal. That should keep them away for a few days at least," Turner explained with a smile as he stood. He offered Whitney a hand to help her stand. "Now, ladies, what would you like to see first? The bookstore?" He winked at Cassie. "Maybe Leeds Street shopping?" he suggested to Whitney. "Or we could even go to the fortuneteller's house if you have any questions." Turner grinned at the girls. He was going to be a good host for the weekend.

As the sunlight peeked through the curtain Cassie rolled over and covered her head. She was nowhere near being used to the night human world. First off, the skinwalkers seemed to run fine on much less sleep. Cassie did not. She needed her full eight hours, or more, and hadn't had a night since being thrown into the weird night human world to get that. And it kind of turned out that night humans lived up to their name. Everything, well almost everything, was running way past nighttime in Cassie's book; she didn't want to be the reason they headed back to the hotel early. In fact, it seemed like the later they were outside, the more people came out. Night humans really were into nightlife, and that didn't mix well with her need for sleep.

She gave up. The pillow didn't even block the annoying sunlight. Squinting at the curtain, Cassie stood and pulled it back, letting the light pour into her room instantly like ripping off a bandage. She squinted a bit and then her eyes adjusted. Turning to the majestic-looking clock hanging on the wall across the room, she saw that it was only two in the afternoon. It was way too early to be awake after turning in at six-thirty in the morning. She got her eight hours, but kind of was looking forward to more like ten or twelve.

The knock at the front door to the sitting room was quiet, but Cassie heard it. She pulled on the robe behind the bedroom door and cracked open the door to look out into the room. Turner was answering the door, and Whitney was sitting at the table, already fully dressed for the day with her hair and makeup perfectly made. Cassie had to wonder if she used her super night human speed to do that.

Cassie had closed the door before Turner was finished allowing the hotel employee bringing food into the front room.

Ignoring her growling stomach, she went to the bathroom to take a shower and get ready for the day. After hopping under the hot water, Cassie remembered that she still didn't have anything new to wear and would have to put back on the grubby clothes she had worn for two days now. Not exactly the best, but what else could she do? Whitney had been having way too much fun with Turner last night to mention that they would need clothes to make it through their trip.

The steaming hot water only made Cassie want to go back to bed. She considered turning it down and shocking herself awake with cold, but that would only lead to a bad mood. What she needed was coffee. Her uncle frowned upon her drinking coffee, but her aunt had her hooked by the time she was thirteen. It did wonders for keeping her awake on late study nights.

After spending way too much time in the shower, Cassie finally relented to getting out and facing the second day of nothing but major confusion. Whitney and Turner seemed to be having a fun time, but Cassie was just as lost as ever. She had hoped they would drop her off at the local library and let her sit among books—books which could have answers—but they insisted she came with them. The only consolation was Turner was actually pretty good about pointing out all the different night humans. She didn't know what each were, but now she at least had a start as to where to look and how to tell them apart, even when they were just in day human form.

Cassie came out of the shower and stopped at the bed which had been made up for her. There on it was a stack of clean clothes. She was going to have to wear the same clothes from the day before, but they were clean enough that she could smell the detergent from where she stood looking at them.

Quickly she slipped into her jeans and olive green T-shirt to hurry out to the food she smelled earlier. Her spirits lifted surprisingly from just clean clothes.

"Hey, sleepyhead," Whitney said as Cassie entered the sitting room.

The couch where Turner had crashed for the night wasn't made up like Cassie's bed. He had insisted that he stay and not leave them alone. He claimed his city was safe, but he said that if anything happened to Cassie, it would be war amongst the night humans. Cassie still couldn't believe that. She was just a normal girl. Who in the world would go to war over her? Nate, most likely, and that kind of made sense. He was always very passionate about everything.

Cassie smiled at Whitney. In her overly organized way, Whitney must have been the one who had her clothes cleaned, and her bed made for her, but it seemed she didn't do the same for Turner.

"Whitney wanted to go back to the fortune-teller now that

it's daytime," Turner explained, motioning for Cassie to get some food from the cart by the door. It was obvious that the cart had been piled high with food which was now more than half gone. Turner had several empty plates in front of him.

"And shopping afterward," Whitney added.

"Yes. And shopping afterward," Turned agreed. He seemed up to do anything they asked. Cassie wondered how he could be such a good guy. To her, he appeared to have just shown up when his friend Devin needed help, and now he was willing to spend his day shopping with her and Whitney just because it was what they wanted.

Cassie took one of the plates and opened the lid. Inside was a stack of steaming pancakes and bacon. She didn't normally have breakfast at two in the afternoon, but she was more than willing to go with the flow after smelling the bacon.

"You really want to go there?" Cassie asked as she sat down with her food. The only memories of seers from her childhood were all frauds. They really couldn't see the future.

Turner stood and walked back over to the cart to grab another plate. He seemed to eat enough for three people. Cassie had no clue how he could look so good after eating that much.

"OJ?" Turner asked Cassie, picking up one of the drinks on the bottom side of the shelf she didn't even notice.

"Any coffee?" Cassie asked, ready for a shot of caffeine.

"Yeah," Turner replied, picking up the coffee carafe and pouring Cassie a hot cup. "Sugar or milk?"

"Just black, and hopefully strong enough to wake me up to keep up with you two," Cassie replied. Turner handed her the warm cup, and she turned back to her friend who hadn't answered yet.

"Well, we were kind of talking while you slept," Whitney began, not looking at Cassie.

"Talking?" Cassie asked, raising an eyebrow at her

friend. It wasn't like Whitney not to look her in the eyes. Whitney was one of the most direct people Cassie knew.

"I told him more about why no one could tell you about night humans while growing up. How everyone thought your father might be a wendigo and all. Turner said the fortune-teller lady can tell you exactly what your father was just by meeting you. She has some sort of seer powers," Whitney quickly explained.

Once again Cassie stared in amazement at her friend. Whitney normally didn't to go telling stuff like that to someone she just met. Yeah, Cassie knew Turner a little bit from the summer, but he still was an outsider. Cassie was at a loss for words.

"I pulled it out of her," Turner interrupted. "I wanted to know why she had to go back so bad, and she said something about needing to know more about your fate after joining the skinwalker clan."

Cassie still didn't know what to say. It was only recently that she was even told why everything was kept from her. No one could or would tell her a thing growing up, and now Whitney was buddy-buddy with Turner. Was it because he was a night human? Did they trust each other more than others?

"Does it even matter now?" Cassie replied. "I'm Nate's mate. I can't exactly get out of it. And besides, could I even be his mate if my father wasn't a skinwalker?"

Whitney shrugged. "You're his mate, but it still matters. It might not matter right now to Than, but it might matter later. Night humans are a mutation. If you have kids, they could turn out to be a wendigo if your father was one, and the coven and clan will reject you then. You kind of need to know."

"But I thought that was all settled because of Nate. My uncle seemed to think me choosing Nate meant I was a skinwalker's child."

Again, Cassie had no clue what to make of it. One time

they were telling her it means something good, and now Whitney is saying that wasn't necessarily so. Cassie tended to believe Whitney more than everyone else. She was the one who had been the most honest with her all along. Cassie glanced over at her friend, who was still studying her food.

"I need to report to my father. I'll be right back," Turner said, excusing himself from the room.

Cassie waited for the door to close before returning her gaze to her friend.

"What else?"

Turner wasn't the only one who had picked up on Whitney's hesitation.

"And I kind of want to see if there's a mate for me," Whitney added quietly, still not raising her eyes.

"Okay," Cassie replied. That made such more sense. Whitney's talk of kids and the clan rejecting Cassie was just a smoke screen, and she understood that now.

Cassie didn't need to see the seer to know that she wasn't one of the wendigo; she knew in her blood. They were bad, and she wasn't. There was no way her father could have been one of them. Cassie wasn't afraid of meeting a seer who could tell her just that.

"Okay?" Whitney asked, finally lifting her head.

"Yeah, sure. We can go there, and I can pretend to care who my father was, and you can pretend to help me by going first," Cassie suggested. That would work.

Whitney grinned at Cassie. After all, they were best friends. Cassie didn't need the answers, but Whitney did. She would sit through an unnecessary meeting for her friend. In fact, she'd do just about anything for Whitney. That's what best friends did. Whitney didn't have anything to worry about. She had Cassie's back on more occasions than Cassie could do anything for her, and she was happy to be finally able to be the one helping.

"Great, let's go right away," Whitney said, tossing her food back on the cart. "I don't want to have to wait until tomorrow again. Turner said the old lady likes to turn in early and hates to stay up late."

Cassie nodded. She could see a weight lifted from Whitney at the thought of finding out her future. Cassie knew what it was like to be an outsider. She had been one her whole life. Her friend wanted answers. At one time she did, too. Now she just wanted a way out and back to her normal night-human-free life. That wasn't going to happen, but that didn't mean Whitney didn't need help.

Whitney grabbed Cassie's arm as Cassie put her half-eaten food back on the tray and dragged her out into the hallway where Turner was leaning against the wall.

"Ready to go?" he asked, looking between the girls.

"Yes," Whitney replied, taking the arm Turner offered her. "Cassie should learn the truth sometime."

Cassie waited for Turner to look away before she rolled her eyes. The truth wasn't all it was cracked up to be.

Turner took the girls on their second tour of town, this time walking in the opposite direction of the bustling city center they were at the night before. The further they walked from the hotel, the quieter it became. Turner talked and kept them busy with stories, but Cassie was tuning him and Whitney out. The night human stuff was too new for Cassie to follow, and the houses they passed here were much more interesting.

It was almost dusk, and lights all over were beginning to turn on. As they passed house after house, Cassie could get a glimpse inside. People were sitting down for a meal, some to end their day and others to begin theirs. Most people in town the night before walked around looking like day humans, but now she could see a variety she never imagined was possible. One eye, three eyes, four legs, tails, horns, some as white as ghosts and others as green as grass. There was such a variety, and it was all different to her. Cassie was so caught up in her window peeking that she didn't notice her friends had stopped talking.

"I suppose this is all new to her now, isn't it?" a shrill, high-pitched voice said, breaking Cassie from her thoughts.

Whitney muffled a laugh as Cassie turned red at being caught looking into people's houses.

"Come, come, young ones," the gray-haired lady who had just spoken added, as she shuffled back into her home.

Cassie closed her eyes to take two deeps breaths and tried to get the red in her face to recede as she followed her friends into the house.

It wasn't what Cassie was expecting at all. She had been to fake and real fortune-tellers over the years on her few travels with her aunt. They always lived in gaudy houses with large neon signs telling you to stop and hear your future. None of them were little gray-haired ladies leading you into what Cassie imagined a grandmother's kitchen would look like. The retro red and white kitchen and dining room had a large table with six chairs at it. There were lacy doilies in the middle of the table, a bowl of fresh baked cookies on top of them, and homemade lemonade waiting in four glasses, as if she had been expecting them all along. Maybe she had.

"Are you enjoying the city?" the old seer asked, plopping down not-so-gracefully since her stiff knees didn't bend as easily as the rest of her.

"Oh, yes. I've never been out of town before; this is great fun. It might be because we have a great host," Whitney added, batting her eyes at Turner. She had tried her best to flirt with him every chance she got. Whitney was always like that. Probably just another reason the girls at school didn't like her. She was quite good at finding those opportunities.

The old lady looked at Whitney as she talked. She nodded along with her, and then closed her eyes for a moment. When she opened them, she looked straight at Cassie. The blue was as clear as the eyes from Cassie's dreams. She often dreamed of blue eyes that clear. She reminded Cassie of her summer trip to the sidhe. They all had those clear, sky-blue eyes.

"I'm not one of them," the lady seemed to respond to Cassie's thoughts.

"You can read minds?" Whitney asked, her face turning red.

"No, child, but I'm sorry to inform you that young master Turner isn't your fated mate. If I were eighty years younger, I'd chase after him, too. No, Turner has a fate that's much larger," the lady responded.

"Hey, now," Turner interrupted her, shoving the whole cookie on his plate into his mouth in one bite. "We've been over this before. No details. I want no details."

He was actually pouting.

Cassie had to laugh. All the bravado was completely gone from Turner, and he was acting like a small child as he pouted. Even like that, he still seemed just so… Turner. She had never met anyone like him and thought the world might be a bit more fun if there were more like him. Cassie would have given anything to be the little sister he claimed she could be with her recent actions.

"Yeah, yeah." The lady patted his hand. "I know. It isn't like you don't do this each time you stop by. But if you'd just let me warn you about next week—"

"Stop," Turner pleaded.

"Fine. But don't say I didn't try," the lady teased him while winking at Cassie. "Most people don't understand our gift is one that's meant to be shared."

"Ours?" Cassie asked.

"The gift of sight," the lady replied. "I know they have tried their best to keep you from coming into your own, but they can't stop fate. That last one the witches had was just too much. They should have listened to me years ago. Oh well. You can lead a horse to water, but you can't make it drink."

Had? As far as Cassie knew, the seer for the witches had been the same one for over fifty years.

"Now onto the fun." The old seer rubbed her hands together. "Go on. Take a cookie."

Cassie looked at Whitney. She shrugged but did as she was told.

"What brings you all here today, besides Master Turner teasing me with his presence once again and refusing to let me tell him his future?" The old lady gingerly lifted her glass of lemonade and took a sip of it.

"We came today to find out who Cassie's father is, but since she's worried about doing this, I figure I could go first," Whitney suggested.

Cassie had to keep from smiling as she nodded along. Whitney didn't just have movie star looks; when she wanted to, she could act just as well as anyone Cassie had seen on the big screen.

The old seer nodded along like she was in on the scheme.

"Yes, yes, that should put Miss Cassie at ease. It's quite hard to be on the receiving end of our gift if you are used to doing it to others. What is your question on this fine afternoon?" She turned to Whitney.

"Hmm. Let's see …" Whitney pretended to think of a question. "How about … You know that all the skinwalkers get a witch that's their mate. Is there one for me, too?"

The old lady reached out quicker than Cassie could have predicted and stopped Whitney from picking her cookie back up. Snatching it from Whitney's hand, she quickly took a bite before handing it back to her. Whitney took the cookie but just held it, giving the old lady the same look that Cassie had on her face.

The seer closed her eyes. "Hmmm. Yes. I see." She nodded to herself.

The girls both looked at Turner. He just grinned and shook his head. He had mentioned that the seer was a bit odd yesterday, but Cassie thought the old-lady house with the plastic-covered couch was the extent of it. It seemed his assessment of odd maybe included her ability to see. Cassie had to look into someone's eyes to see their past, but others had to do different things, such as hold their hand, touch someone's head, or whatnot. Eating their cookie was one Cassie had not heard of.

The old woman finally opened her eyes and looked directly at Whitney. The sky blue color was now clouded with white clouds, almost giving her eyes a cataract appearance.

"You've already met your mate, but until you know the truth of your real father, you won't see them as your mate," the old lady said in an eerily clear voice. She blinked and her eyes were back to their normal color.

"Real father?" Whitney asked.

The old lady shrugged. "I don't know what it means any more than you do. My sight isn't as clear as hers."

The old lady nodded to Cassie, but she had no clue what the woman was talking about. Cassie's "sight" was picking up on emotions, or even seeing something someone had done. She hadn't seen the future or, at least, she couldn't on purpose. She could barely control seeing people's thoughts and pasts.

"Now your fortune."

Cassie tried to take her cookie back but was too slow. For an old person, the seer was extremely quick. The seer took a bite and began to chew slowly.

"Your question?"

"I don't have any questions today," Cassie replied.

There was no way she was going to ask about her own father now that Whitney got her cryptic reply. Yes, the seer had answered that Whitney would have a mate and had met him, but she just dropped a bomb on her with the *real* father bit. Basically, the old seer was saying that Whitney's father wasn't her father, which had to be impossible. Cassie had seen baby pictures of Whitney with her dad.

Cassie didn't need any information she didn't want to know being dropped on her right now. She could barely keep up with all the new things in her life as it was. She didn't need to know anything about her father now.

The old lady closed her eyes and nodded again, even though Cassie hadn't asked a question.

Her clouded eyes opened back up, and she looked at Cassie.

"Answers will be coming for you, though not from me. All I can say is that your father wasn't ever committed to one clan. You, therefore, don't belong to one clan. You're a free agent in their world, and no one will know what to do with you. You'll either connect them or destroy them."

Yep, Cassie *really* didn't need to know that.

CHAPTER 3

"**You do realize** that there's a speed limit?" Cassie asked as they zoomed up the mountainside leading back home.

She wasn't looking forward to all the noise that would come when they passed over the top. Whitney had explained that the noise was something that came with being alpha. Nate had constant contact with his clan, and being bonded to him made her part of all of that. Cassie didn't want a mate, or to be connected. She liked her head quiet.

"Sorry," Whitney replied. She slowed down by only a couple of miles an hour, therefore essentially keeping the same pace racing home. "I always thought my mother's fancy talking was because she was hiding something, but I have a different father? How is that possible? How didn't I know that? Why didn't they tell me?"

Whitney was back to her ranting. Cassie didn't know how to reply. She didn't have parents, but Whitney's possibly false father meant the world to her. If Dave didn't turn out to be her father, Whitney would be crushed. Whitney even looked like Dave. Cassie was beyond confused.

As they neared the top of the peak, Cassie paused to hold her breath. Good-bye, silence. It had been nice.

They passed the spot where it all went away when they left on their trip, and there was nothing. No voices. No headache. Nothing.

"Something's not right," Cassie said. She didn't want the constant hum back, but the silence felt wrong being that close to home.

'Cassie, turn around and leave before they feel you,'

Nate said into Cassie's mind.

'What's going on?' Cassie replied. Nate was so set not to have her leave just days ago, and now he was trying to keep her from coming back. It didn't make sense.

"Nate says we should go back to where we came from," Cassie told Whitney.

"He just told me the same thing." Whitney continued to drive toward home. "I told him 'screw you'."

Cassie laughed. No wonder he sounded a bit upset. Cassie knew that he didn't like people disagreeing with him, but Whitney was beyond disagreeable.

"Then we're still heading home?" Cassie asked. The alpha could command Whitney, but it seemed like Nate couldn't.

"Oh, my mother isn't going to get away with lies this time," Whitney muttered as she sped up again.

They made it home in record time since Whitney didn't drive the speed limit for any part of the trip. Cassie wondered what Nate was doing now, but she didn't have a clue what it all meant. He hadn't answered any of the questions she had been silently communicating the whole time they had been driving. Beyond telling her to leave, he had stayed quiet and so had the clan. Something was off.

Main Street wasn't empty when they arrived, but it was odd. Cassie got a gut feeling that maybe Nate was right after all. They shouldn't have returned. The place was filled with strangers. Not a single person walking down the street was recognizable. The men—both young and old—who walked around were all new to Cassie. It wasn't odd to see one or two new faces as people traveled through town, but there was no one Cassie knew. And they were all guys. Not a single woman walked among them. Whitney slowed down to the stoplight in the middle of downtown.

"I think possibly something is going on," Cassie said as she looked in front of her. Still no one she knew. Cassie had grown up there. There should have been at least someone she knew walking around. This many strangers meant something was up.

"Oh, I think more than maybe, and I don't get the feeling we're welcome here." Whitney nodded her head behind her.

Cassie turned around to see several of the men transforming into the monsters that still haunted her dreams. Long, grotesque arms with claws the size of kitchen knives, long snouts with teeth dripping saliva waiting to bite into them, and thin, triangle-shaped fury bodies perched on backward facing legs. Yep, her nightmare was coming alive behind them.

"Yeah, not exactly a welcoming party," Cassie replied, trying not to look back at them. She didn't need more nightmares. "My house is closer."

Whitney nodded as she watched in her rearview mirror. The monsters weren't running, but they were slowly stalking toward them.

"Remember how you thought those racing lessons were a waste of time?" Whitney asked, watching her mirror and the stoplight at the same time.

Whitney had asked for her sixteenth birthday to have car lessons on a race track. Her father, whom she loved dearly, agreed it was handy to know how to really drive a car and talked her mother into it. Cassie and Owen laughed the whole time, but it turned out Whitney was actually quite good at driving and driving fast. Probably her night human reflexes, but whatever it was, Cassie hoped she still had it in her.

"Time to show me that you have been practicing," Cassie added.

Whitney looked back at the guys behind them.

"Three ... two ... one," Whitney counted. On one, there was a thump when one of the creatures leaped from behind them to in front of them

Cassie wouldn't say she could tell the monsters apart. They were large with dark-colored arms which hung almost to the ground past their backward-slanted knees. The fur covering much of their bodies could have been different colors, but Cassie wasn't about to sit around and study them. They had made it very clear before that they wanted her for something, and she wasn't ready to be monster food. The one standing in front of her glared at her with his beady, red eyes from beneath its shoulder-length mane of black hair. He gave a slight smile to show his elongated teeth, which matched the razor-sharp claws Cassie was way too familiar with. Cassie shivered. She had a good feeling this was the one she knew—the one who had already once tried to kill her.

"*Go!*" Cassie shouted at Whitney as she stared at the monster before her.

Whitney didn't wait to think more, but stepped on the gas and aimed right for the creature of Cassie's nightmares. The monster had a look of shock as he had to jump out of the way. He must not have expected the girls to fight back, but if that was the case, he had another thing coming.

She whipped off the main street to a road lined with cars. The group of monsters chasing them had to group closer together, almost forming a line as they followed. Whitney continued to drive through a roundabout way to get to Cassie's home, losing one or two of the monsters on every turn, but some kept joining the group.

"Your aunt better know how to get these things away from us," Whitney commented as Cassie had to grab the handle above her head on another sharp turn.

They had just driven past Owen's house, and it was as dark as the rest on the street. Cassie got a sinking feeling in her stomach. This didn't look good. Something was off.

'*What is going on here?*' Cassie asked across the bond of emptiness, hoping Nate was back and would tell her what to do or even what had happened.

"Nate's not answering," Cassie commented, slamming against her car door on the last turn.

"He's not answering me either. That means he's either really busy or—" Whitney didn't get to finish. She slowed only momentarily but then continued past Cassie's house.

They both knew it wasn't a good idea to stop. Cassie's house was just as dark and void of people as the rest of the homes. The only difference was it looked like someone blew a hole through the front of the house. Claw marks were all over the doors, and Cassie could only imagine how many of the monsters following them had attacked her house.

"Guess we need to try my house," Whitney replied, finally getting back her fighting spirit.

"Yeah. Your mother would never let anyone attack your little brother." Cassie replied.

Whitney began to whip around another block and kept up her racecar driver pace. They needed somewhere to hide and soon. The monsters behind them seemed impatient.

"I think I see something running in the woods," Cassie commented as a large, black shape kept pace with the car.

"Shoot. I thought we lost that one back at your house," Whitney replied. She couldn't turn away from the woods as her house sat on the edge of it.

Whitney pulled up to her house and automatically went into the driveway. The monsters were only half a block behind them. Cassie glanced up at the dark house. It looked as vacant as all of them in town.

"Mom?" Whitney yelled, opening her window a crack.

The only thing Cassie heard in reply were the monsters that were too close for comfort.

"We need to get out of here," Cassie commented, looking behind them. Whitney had a long driveway, and they were now at the far end of it. The monsters all stopped as a car pulled down the road and blocked the mouth of the driveway.

"Shit," Whitney said under her breath. She wasn't one to swear, and her mother hopefully wasn't home, or Whitney would be grounded for months.

"What do we do?" Cassie asked.

She hated the feeling that she didn't have time to fight back. Cassie had seen the sidhe over the summer and saw their version of magic. They were warriors and had turned witch magic into a way of fighting. Cassie promised herself the next time she had a break to catch her breath from running from monsters she was going to learn how to do that. It seemed like her survival depended on fighting back.

A large brown bear stepped out of the woods.

"When I tell you to climb out of the car, you get out and close your eyes. I'm going to transform partially and pick you up to run," Whitney explained. "Help just arrived."

"Help?" Cassie asked, staring at the wild bear in front of them. It wasn't even looking at them. It was looking at the monsters.

"Your uncle," Whitney replied. "Though I have no idea how or why he's fully transformed. It isn't a full moon tonight."

Cassie glanced behind them. The monsters were all snarling as someone exited the car behind them. They didn't even turn around and seemed to be waiting for the new person to join them.

"I think we better go soon," Cassie added.

Bear John gave out a growl that made Cassie shake in her seat. She sure hoped the large creature was her uncle.

"Now," Whitney replied, not giving Cassie more time to worry about it.

Cassie threw open her door and jumped out of the car. She barely had time to close her eyes when she felt Whitney's arms scoop her up and begin running. Wind whipped through Cassie's hair. Whitney was right. There was no way Cassie would be able to keep her eyes open as her friend ran through the woods—it was faster than riding with the windows open in the car during the summer. Before she could complain, Cassie was standing upright again, and Whitney was beside her.

"We need to put up your protection spell around the cabin quick before they track us here," Whitney explained. "I sure hope you left some of it here."

Cassie nodded and ran after her friend to the cabin.

"It didn't exactly stop them the last time," Cassie complained.

Whitney pulled the door open. "That's because you didn't know what you needed protection from. It's different now. You can't put a spell on something you don't believe in."

Whitney stepped inside the darkened cabin with Cassie right behind her. A pop sounded from in front of them, and Cassie only had time to turn to the noise before she noticed her friend dropping to the ground beside her. A handful of glowing dust magically lit up the room momentarily, and Cassie found herself frozen in place.

"Sorry we had to do it this way, but you'll thank me in the morning," a male voice said.

Cassie couldn't move as she wanted to squint in the night to see who the person was. The voice was familiar, but she had no clue as she couldn't see.

She thought of a counter spell and repeated the words over and over again in her head. She needed to be free, and she wanted nothing to do with the monsters chasing her. They would eat her alive if they found her in her cabin frozen. She and Whitney were sitting ducks, waiting to be eaten. Cassie had to get them free.

"Stop," the guy said as if he knew what she was doing and could see her move in the dark.

Cassie had only freed two fingers from the spell as they twitched to motion. She needed more time. Whoever made the spell was powerful, but she was even more so. She had to get away. The guy with her had no clue the monsters were chasing her, or worse, he could be with them. She needed to be free. Cassie pushed all her energy into the counter spell.

"Cassie, stop that. You need to come with me," he told

her, moving closer. "We have Nate, and if I don't return with you tonight, your cousin is going to kill him."

Upon hearing that, Cassie stopped casting her spell. They had Nate. That's why he told her to go away. Whitney said Nate couldn't talk back only if he was unconscious or dead. He wasn't dead yet, but would be soon if she didn't stop. Could she believe the guy speaking? Moving closer, he reached up and touched her face. Now he was only an arm's length away and standing close enough to the light pouring through the door for Cassie to see. Jared stared at her as he waited for her to believe him. He moved into the moonlight, which was now shining brightly.

"Look in my eyes if you need to trust me, but I would never lie to you. They have him and plan to kill him if they can't find you," Jared explained. "They've only kept him this long to try to get to you. He wouldn't tell us where you were."

Cassie looked at him. He was being completely honest with her. She could see memories of the day and how her cousin was holding Nate captive. Nate was strapped to a table with electrodes on him to shock him constantly and keep him subdued. His whole upper body covered in cuts that varied from little shallow ones to a few deeper stabs showed how badly he'd been beaten.

"Jack will kill him," Jared told her, waiting for her to agree with him.

His eyes told her what she needed to know. Cassie stopped resisting the spell. She needed Jared to take her back if that meant they would spare Nate. Whether she wanted to be his mate or not didn't matter at this point. She wanted him to live, and that was all she was worried about right now.

Jared moved closer and wrapped his arms around her waist. He touched her forehead with more magic, and she instantly felt sleep hit her.

The morning light was seeping through the curtains by the time Cassie woke. She stretched as she lay in bed. She felt smooth satin sheets beneath her and instantly opened her eyes. Sitting up, she rubbed her eyes, trying to remember where she was or what had happened the night before. The half-opened window curtains showed off the deep purple and green colors of the room. Cassie closed her eyes and rubbed her head again. She was drawing a blank as to where she was or what she had been doing.

Magical residue was still on her forehead as she rubbed it. Cassie pulled her fingers back and looked at them closely. She couldn't exactly see the magic, but it was more like she could feel it. Her fingers rubbed it back and forth. It wasn't a weak potion, but it wasn't familiar. She could name most of the students in school based on how they made their potions, and likely even their families because it was all relatively passed down from generation to generation, but this was new. This was from someone she hadn't met before.

"Your cousin said that would wear off in a couple of hours, but it's been over eight," Jared said from across the room. He stood and walked into the pale purple light the curtains had brightened the room to.

Cassie rolled more of it between her fingers. It was a strong potion, and anyone that knew even a little bit of magic wouldn't have said only a couple hours.

"This wasn't made to end in only a couple hours. He lied to you," she replied, staying in her bed as the rush of memories came back to her.

Monsters had been chasing her and Whitney. Her uncle as a bear helped them escape. They went to the cabin, and Jared did something to Whitney.

"Where is she?" Cassie asked. The last detail in her memories came back, and she covered her mouth. Jared had said if she didn't go with him quick enough they were going to kill Nate. "Did you guys kill him?"

"Whitney is fine. I had to get you back here to protect

you from her," Jared began his explanation.

"I don't need protection from her. She would never hurt me, but you guys … You've proved more than once that you'd like me dead."

Jared slowly moved forward, silent as a panther.

"No one will ever try to hurt you again. If they do, they have me to deal with," Jared explained, not exactly answering any questions.

"And Nate?" Cassie whispered. She wasn't afraid of Jared; he had been nice to her the last time she had visited her cousin. She was afraid for Nate. He said they were planning to kill him, and the memory she saw showed he wasn't in too good of shape.

"He's fine now that you're here," Jared replied with a shrug, like he didn't care at all.

"And Whitney?" Cassie asked. She was obviously alone in the huge, purple-glowing room.

"Ryder is watching over her," Jared replied.

"Ryder?" Cassie asked, starting to fear for her friend.

"He won't hurt her," Jared explained, making it close enough to sit on the edge of the bed. "He's just watching over her until she changes. Then he'll take her to the woods and let her go, just like the rest. We're not killers like the coven teaches. Once everyone had transformed, we caught them and took them out to the woods for the safety of everyone in town."

Cassie looked at Jared. He was hiding nothing and completely open with her, but making no sense. Whitney had explained the skinwalker thing was like werewolves in movies—they changed into their full animals on the full moon. She was right in that the moon was bright last night, but not a full moon. Was Ryder watching over her for days, waiting for the full moon? That really made no sense.

"How do you feel?" Jared asked, reaching up for her face but putting his hand back down.

"Feel? Like someone did a spell on me, but not the first

time. Why?" Cassie asked.

"You were out longer than I thought you would be and you were thrashing around the whole time. I thought I did something to hurt you."

She shrugged. "Don't worry about it. It wasn't the first, and it won't be the last. I think the last spell put on me was last week by the coven. It happens. It doesn't feel good, and eventually, they wear off. That's life as a witch." Cassie had no idea why she was reassuring him.

Jared nodded and still looked her over. Cassie swung her legs off the bed and finally noticed the chain around her left ankle.

"What is..." Cassie stared at the chain. She was chained to the bed. That was a new one. The coven never had to restrain people physically because they just used magic, but she got the feeling here was a bit different.

"You can't be left alone right now. The clan doesn't trust you. Once you are bonded to me, they will let you come and go as you please, but until then..." Jared directed his gaze over to the window as he spoke. He seemed a bit embarrassed.

"Until then you'll keep me chained up?" she finished for him. He nodded.

Jared continued to stare away in shame. Cassie would have laughed if she wasn't annoyed by everything. She had met him last week, and he was the only one who didn't scare the crap out of her. In fact, it was quite the opposite. She was more than intrigued by him then and still didn't know what to think. Jared was a mystery to her, but his shy side was kind of cute, so different from all the guys she knew growing up. He was with her cousin, and from what she could tell they were the bad guys, at least from how Whitney explained it. The wendigo attacked humans and drank their blood. The skinwalkers protected the humans from the wendigo. Cassie, being human, got the feeling it was a no-brainer which side she was on. But Jared? He was different. His eyes weren't the hardened stare she got from her cousin or his brother, Ryder. He didn't look at the world like he wanted to conquer it. He wasn't trying to hide behind a smile like Jack. Jared was real, and even if she knew almost nothing about him, she could tell. He wasn't bad.

"Can I see Whitney and Nate?" she asked.

"I don't know if Whitney is still here, but we can go see," Jared replied. Reaching down, he unlocked the chain from her foot. "Please don't wander away from me. Until we are bonded, some might still see you as the enemy. I can't protect you if you run away from me."

He was completely honest and sincere, but Cassie still cringed. She was already bonded, and she needed to get away before anyone found out. People could only bond to one person. Until she understood the situation better, she would play by his rules, but that was only until she found a way out. She had already played this game with Nate's henchmen that were protecting her. Once she knew where Whitney and Nate were, she would see how to get out. They were not sticking around; no matter how much Jared kept saying she would be safe, she got the very distinct feeling she would never be safe with the wendigo.

Jared led the way to what Cassie expected was a door to a hallway. It turned out it led to a stairwell. The open metal stairs spiraled down to the room below. Cassie stepped into an immaculately clean guy's room.

"Umm …" Cassie didn't know what to say.

Jared ran his hands through his chocolate-brown hair, which was long enough it was curling around his ears, but nowhere as long as his twin, Ryder, who could pull his blond hair into a ponytail.

"Yeah. Sorry. Tradition and all." He shrugged his explanation.

"Tradition?" Cassie asked, trying to catch his eyes as he avoided hers.

"You've heard of mother-in-law suites?" he asked. Cassie

nodded but had no idea what he meant by it. "Well, this is sort of a mate's suite."

Cassie froze in her tracks. It had been bad enough when Nate chose her as his mate without her agreeing, but now Jared, too? And he was going to chain her up in a tower on top of it? She needed Owen around to crack some fairy tale joke and make it not feel as real as it did. Her life was a freaking fairy tale at the moment.

"Um, excuse me?" Cassie replied. "This is the twenty-first century. Not exactly legal to chain girls up in rooms and force them to marry you, you know."

"I know. I know," Jared quickly replied. "And I said I'm sorry. This is all clan stuff. Sometimes I don't get a say in things, especially tradition. It wasn't meant to be taking you as a prisoner. Most of the women who are chosen as mates are more than excited to get treated like a princess."

"Yeah. Sorry. I'm not most people. I'd rather go back home and pretend the whole night human world stuff doesn't exist," Cassie replied. "And it's very insulting." She pointed up to the room with the chain on the bed. *Chained to a bed in a tower? How much more cliché could they get?*

"I know. I'm sorry," Jared apologized again. "Once the clan sees you aren't going to harm anyone I promise we will make some changes. Right now, they're all afraid of you being here uncommitted to a wendigo."

"Then why not take me home and let me live my life the way I want?" Cassie suggested snarkily. Why couldn't her life just be easy?

She wasn't normally brash, especially with strangers, but something about Jared felt familiar. He didn't feel like a stranger. He felt much like Owen; she was now beginning to worry about her other best friend.

"I'm sorry, Cassie. I truly am, but you can't go back, to your home or to your life before you knew about night humans. You were destined to be here at this moment. We can't change things like that. We can't change what we are born into and what we're meant to do." He began walking to the door on the left side of the room.

"What happened here?" Cassie finally asked. "Why can't I go home?" He made it seem final.

"I was pretty sure my brother said you drove past your uncle's place." Jared didn't turn around. "When John transformed, he destroyed it. There's no home to go back to at the moment."

Jared reached for the door handle, but Cassie stopped him by placing a hand on his arm.

"What happened here?" Cassie asked, looking up into his eyes.

Jared just stared back at her. She caught a jumble of images—people turned into animals, witches screaming, and then some of herself as a kid. It was an odd assortment that left more questions than answers. Jared closed his eyes and cocked his head to the side, like some of those images weren't meant to be seen.

"We need to go down to the barn now if you want to see your friend off. She transformed about an hour ago, it seems. Ryder is packing her up to release her." Jared opened his eyes and looked back at Cassie. His tone immediately changed. "I'll explain it all when we get a moment alone. You wanted to see your friend, and I want you to see we didn't harm her. We were really keeping you safe. She could have turned at any moment once she came back into town, and then you would have been stuck in a car or house with a cougar. That wouldn't have been safe. All the skinwalkers are going feral when they turn."

"That's not possible. She doesn't have a mate. She can't turn until the full moon, and that's over a week away."

"I promise I'll explain more, but they are hauling her to the truck. I doubt Ryder will wait for us. He doesn't exactly like to listen to me." Jared held out his hand, like she was to take it. "Please just play along that you're considering being my mate. It'll make everyone else a bit calmer and easier to get through."

Cassie tried to hide her shock that he could see that she was far from sold on the idea. She had only just met him a week ago, and now it was like he could read her face and her mind at the same time.

"Just pretend for now and make your choices later, after you see your friends."

She took his outstretched hand. Again, it felt familiar. How could someone she just met feel like she had known him her whole life? It had to be because he was Owen's cousin. It was almost like a bit of Owen was there with her.

"And Owen or my aunt? Are they okay?" Cassie asked. She knew where her uncle was and that they had Nate and Whitney. She still didn't know about Owen or her aunt.

"Owen was one of the first to transform. He's running around the woods somewhere. He's fine just like the rest of the skinwalkers. They're just not human anymore," Jared said quietly.

"And my aunt?"

Jared led them outside the room into the hallway. There was a door cracked open across the hall that looked like a messy mirror image of Jared's room. Jared paused.

"I can't discuss that out here. Other ears might be listening," he told her, pleading with his eyes for her to drop the subject.

Cassie didn't see another soul in the empty hallway, but night humans had much better hearing. She dropped it... for now.

The house wasn't as large as Cassie expected, or at least, it didn't take long to leave it. Down the hallway from Jared's room was a mudroom which led outside. Cassie wasn't even sure what the rest of the house looked like, but they were immediately outside, and Jared was pulling her quickly down the hill on a walkway that might have been paved or cement at one time, but was beyond repair at the moment.

Cassie didn't ask any more questions but kept a lookout

around her. They were in the woods, but it wasn't by her cousin's place because it was much hillier. She didn't have a sense of direction to where town was. The brush was thick, and she was sure any leaving outside would be impossible without her friends to lead the way. She never would be able to find civilization again with it the way it was. She needed to find a way to free her friends, and then they would all be able to leave together.

The path turned and opened up to a large parking area and barn. It looked eerily similar to the barn at her cousin's house where Jack held her friends captive and tried to kidnap her.

"They come with the places around here?" Cassie joked to cover her growing dread.

Several cars were parked outside the barn. Ryder yelled at someone.

Jared led Cassie around the larger van blocking her view of the other vehicles. Behind it was Ryder next to a small pickup truck that had its cargo area filled. He was busy talking to someone. Ryder abruptly stopped as they came into view and he smiled up at them.

"You made it in time to say good-bye," he said cheerfully.

Cassie had to do a double look at him. She had met him before, and he was beyond scary. He seemed like the embodiment of the evil Whitney told her the wendigo was, but now Cassie didn't feel that from him. It was almost like he was a different person. Cassie knew that wasn't true, but it still felt that way. He was still the same guy who gave her nightmares, and still the same one that was chasing them the night before, at least on the outside.

"We got her all packed up, but don't get too close. She's a feisty one," Ryder continued.

He grabbed the edge of a blanket that was thrown over something in the back of the truck they were standing by. Inside a small cage with just enough room for her to stand was Whitney in her cat form. Cassie had assumed wrongly that Whitney was the tiger she had met when the crazy night human world first began, but she wasn't. She was about a third of the size of Nate in his tiger form and a tawny color with a light black dusting of hair around her mouth and above her eyes. Cassie had never seen a cougar in the wild, but she had seen one in the zoo before. It was strange to know it was her best friend inside the cat.

The cat hissed and scratched at the bars in Ryder's direction. Whitney was beautiful as a cat, but scary when she was looking at Ryder.

"I don't think she likes you much, brother," Jared commented, holding tight to Cassie's hand to keep her from getting any closer to her friend.

"I might have asked her to undress before turning purely to save her from ruining her clothing and all." Ryder grinned.

Cat Whitney hissed at him, claws scraping on the metal. It was as if she understood what he said and was beyond mad.

"What are you going to do with her?" Cassie asked, still watching her friend. Whitney turned around in the cage and lay down, keeping her eyes on Ryder.

"We trapped each one that was dangerous in town and took them out to Beck's park," Ryder explained. "The woods at Beck's butts right up against the Morin State Park. They should be safe there, as there's no hunting allowed."

"You're really just setting them free?" Cassie asked.

Ryder looked at her with a scrunched-up face. "What else are we going to do with them?"

Cassie shrugged. "Whitney said you guys are set to kill each other every chance you get. Something about a war over territory." Cassie wasn't exactly sure what the history behind the two groups was, but she was sure that the wendigo weren't good guys. Only good guys would take the enemy to the woods and let them go.

Ryder laughed. "There's no territory to fight over. The witches are all gone, and all the skinwalkers are animals. Well, all except your former mate. There's no one to fight with. The town and all in it are ours now."

The guy from before came back out to the car and tossed keys to Ryder.

"We'll be back in an hour," Ryder said to his brother before climbing into the driver's side of the truck.

The car slowly backed up and then began to drive away. Cassie watched her friend, and she could have sworn that her friend was watching her, not very feral. Inside that animal was Whitney. Cassie needed to find out why and how they were keeping everyone in their changed form. She couldn't have help from her friend if she were now a cougar. Everyone she had ever known growing up was gone. Cassie needed to find answers.

CHAPTER 4

After Whitney's departure, Jared led Cassie into the side door of the barn. It was unnervingly similar to the barn she had been in only a week ago when the wendigo were holding Nate and Whitney captive. Nate was the only one this time. He was tied up by his ankles and wrists in a semi-standing position, covered head to toe in cuts that ranged from one-inch gashes on his arms to a long, at least six-inch, cut on his chest. He looked up immediately as they entered and his fierce glare turned to worry when he saw Cassie.

"You shouldn't be here," Nate told her, his voice raspy.

"You said he was fine." Cassie dropped Jared's hand and rushed over to Nate.

"He is fine," Jack replied, stepping into the room from the doorway behind Nate.

Cassie froze only a foot away from Nate. She didn't exactly leave Jack on good terms the week before. Actually, she hoped that her skinwalker friends would have done enough damage to keep him out of commission for a long time. Jack was family she had never known growing up, and now she didn't care to learn anything more about him. She had seen it in his eyes. He was the evil Whitney had warned her about.

Nate's head snapped up, and he glared at Jack, who smiled back at him.

"I've always wanted to test the mating bond. Is it like a blood connection? Will you bleed if I cut him?" Jack commented, reaching out and picking up a piece of Cassie's hair. Nate growled at the same time that Jack was suddenly thrown across the room.

Jared stood between Cassie and Jack. "You'd do best to keep your hands off her," he warned Jack.

Rising, Jack wiped his hands off on his pants. He gave a lazy smile to Jared.

"I would never do anything to actually harm Cassie. After all, she's family." Jack grinned. "I was just curious how far the bond goes between mates. No harm." Jack held his hand up in surrender, yet his eyes said he wanted to really know the answer.

"You are going to leave my property and go home, Jack," Jared ordered him.

Jack's eyes flashed with anger. Jared didn't seem intimidated as he stared back at him.

"Mark my words. You are making a mistake," Jack told him. "You need me here to keep him drained and controlled. The minute I'm gone, he'll break free and guess who he'll attack first?"

"You can disagree all you want. I'm the one in charge. We do things my way." Jared kept his back to Cassie and Nate, but Cassie could feel the authority pour off him.

"You can't make an omelet without breaking a few eggs, you know. You're going to have to get your hands dirty sometime." Jack backed up to the door, never turning his back to Jared.

"Not this way," Jared replied, watching Jack with hawk-like eyes. There was something more that wasn't being said between them, but Cassie had no clue what. It was as if she came into the middle of a conversation she wasn't meant to hear.

"Your loss, man." Jack shrugged and slipped out the door.

Jared took a deep breath before turning around. "He was supposed to just watch over Nate and not let him go," he explained to Cassie. "He was never supposed to touch him. That, he did on his own."

"And enjoyed it," Nate added.

Jared shrugged, obviously not surprised by Nate's words. Cassie wasn't too surprised either. Her cousin scared her as much as the wendigo.

"You can have a few minutes alone," Jared told Cassie. "To be sure he's being kept safe. I promise you we aren't here to hurt him. We are waiting for him to change to set him free like everyone else."

Cassie nodded to Jared but didn't take her eyes off Nate. The smaller cuts were halfway gone, and the large one was already smaller. His super night human healing was coming into play. Cassie still felt bad. She was upstairs sleeping peacefully while her deranged cousin was having fun cutting up Nate. It wasn't exactly a fair situation.

The door clicked as Jared left the barn.

Nate watched the door like he expected Jared to come right back. Cassie didn't wait, choosing to inspect the cords around his wrists and legs. They were tied tightly, and she needed something sharp to cut them. Glancing back to the table near the doorway where Jack entered, she saw there were knives of all shapes and sizes. Cassie hated to think how they had been used, but took one anyway. She cut the rope off Nate's right wrist first, just barely missing his skin. Her hands shook as she worked, but she wasn't ready to talk. *He was being tortured.*

Nate covered her hand with his own as she tried to cut free his second wrist.

"I'll do that," he offered, taking the knife from her. With much better precision, Nate cut through the bonds on his wrist and then legs.

Nate stepped down from the almost vertical table to the ground before he fell to his knees, dropping the knife in the process. Cassie jumped down to try to catch him, but he weighed almost twice as much as she did, so it wasn't going to work. They tumbled to the ground together.

"Sorry about that. I prefer to be a bit more graceful, but

it's been a long two days," Nate remarked from his spot on the floor beneath Cassie. He grinned up at her, but Cassie knew it was strained. The cuts were still all over his half-clothed body.

"Why don't you just transform?"

Whitney had explained that when they got hurt in one form or the other, they could transform into the other kind and be instantly healed since the process of transforming put everything back together again.

"I would, but there's something about your crazy cousin. It's like he wants me to do so, and if that's what he wants, it can't be good."

Cassie nodded as she tried to push herself up from Nate. He quickly grabbed ahold of her and kept her pressed to him on the ground.

"If I had any energy, I would take advantage of this. You'll have to thank your cousin for keeping me drained." Nate's eyes sparkled with mischief and made Cassie's stomach do flip flops.

"Let me up," Cassie ordered. "You're injured, and I shouldn't be squishing you, you can't even stand."

Nate laughed while Cassie stared at him in shock. He had been a prisoner for at least two days where her crazy cousin was torturing him, and yet his first bit of freedom and he was lying on the ground laughing.

When Nate loosened his grip, Cassie slid off him, and he pushed himself up to sitting next to her with a bit of effort.

"So about escaping ..." Cassie glanced at the doorway Jared left from.

"Not going to happen without a little magic for me," Nate commented, following her gaze.

"Magic?" Cassie asked. She wasn't sure what sort of spell would help, but at least he knew.

Nate laughed again. "I didn't mean literally. I meant I'm in no condition to run from those monsters, or to fight them when they come chasing you. I need a bit of time, and blood would be nice to get my energy back."

"Was Jack draining you?" Cassie asked, finally realizing what he had said and that even the small cuts were places which would bleed a lot.

"Yeah. Pretty much about the only universal way to make a night human weaker is to take their blood. We all live on blood, night or day humans. It's just that night humans can't make their own like day humans. We run out and have to take more from regular people. Keep a night human drained of blood and they can't fight back."

"Can I help with that?" Cassie asked.

After all, she was a day human, and she was more than willing to give a little blood away if it meant he would carry her off to someplace safe and away from the monsters outside the barn.

"I can't let you. If anyone out there smells your blood, we'll have a room full of wendigo before I can even recover. It isn't safe, no matter how tempting your offer is. And it's tempting. When I'm recovered from all this, can you offer again sometime?" He was grinning at her and, based his jokes, he was okay.

Nate put a hand out for Cassie. He was now propped against the same table he had been tied to for who knew how long. Cassie took his hand, and he pulled her into his lap.

'I'll get you out of here once I'm sure it's safer to be outside the walls than in. I'm pretty sure by what we just saw that Jared won't let anyone harm you. You're safer with him for now until I can talk more with everyone else,' Nate explained silently.

'Wait.' Cassie pulled back from him. *'I've been trying to talk to you since we got back like this. How come it didn't work?'*

'I cut our bond temporarily when Jack was draining me. Our bond isn't just mental. If something happens to me, it happens to you. Luckily, to keep the coven from finding out,

your aunt put a spell on me which allows me to make it temporarily disappear. I've been coming back to check on you every few hours, when I don't have cuts that will transfer to you.'

He was right. She could feel him every now and then, even if he didn't speak. And she could feel everything now. It was all clearer. Nate was weaker than he was letting on. She would scold him, but he was being strong for her. He could feel her worry as much as she could feel his lack of energy. She felt inside him. It was strange, but a bit comforting that he was still there. She had felt alone before. Then it dawned on her. The other voices were all gone. There was still silence. The clan was gone.

'What happened?' Cassie looked up at him. Nate pulled Cassie close so that she could lay her head on him. She couldn't see his face, but had a feeling that was exactly what he was doing it for.

'I don't know exactly. Right after you left town, I was outside my parents' place, trying to track you with our bond. It happened then. My mother just disappeared. I mean vanished into thin air. Without her around to stabilize my dad, he turned into a tiger. I went into town to try to get help, but it was happening all around town. The witches were just gone.'

Cassie was able to see his memories as he talked, and it was like he was narrating a movie. His dad was a large tiger just like Nate. She watched him transform, and saw Nate running to open doors as his father found a way out of the house. Nate rushed into town and saw the animals pouring out of the houses.

'I noticed that the teens without mates were not changing, so we rounded up everyone we could. Witchlings were still around. Only people pledged to a mate were missing. We hid at the school. Then I went to find your uncle when I saw it happen.'

The movie changed to her house, the one she was raised

in, as it blew into pieces and a very angry bear ran out of it. It took only a blink, and anyone could have missed it, but Cassie saw it. Her aunt was riding her uncle as they ran away.

'I went back to the school but was too late. All the young skinwalkers were changing into their full animal, too, and the wendigo were at the school rounding up the witchlings. It's impossible to change without a full moon for the young skinwalkers. I have no clue how they did it. I only got close enough to hear your cousin promise them that they would be safe, but we see what safe means to him.'

The school was emptied of animals, and some were even trapped. Nate stayed in the shadows and watched. There was nothing he could do to help, and it was driving him crazy to just watch. But he was all alone. No one else was left. The older clan members had been the first to leave. Now the younger ones all changed also, and the witches were taken or disappeared. Nate had no clue where they were at all.

'Everyone really is gone?' Cassie asked. Her head was against his chest, and she could hear his heartbeat. It was reassuring that he wasn't a dream and she wasn't alone. Nate was with her.

'I don't know. I was standing there one minute watching, and then next twitching on the ground. I learned skinwalkers are susceptible to Tasers, and Tasers hurt worse than you can imagine.'

'What do we do?' Cassie asked, yawning. How in the world could she be tired? She just woke up.

'We play their game until we know more of what's going on. We can't make a plan without getting more details.' Nate rubbed her head as she closed her eyes. *'I don't know what's going on, but we will find out. We just have to be patient.'*

'Why the heck am I sleepy?'

'Sorry, my fault. When the bond opens up, we use each other's energy. I must be lower than I thought. Sleep and you will feel better.'

'And what about you?' Cassie was struggling to keep her eyes open.

'I'll watch over you. And I'll keep my ears open. There's something going on here. The wendigo weren't there when my mom disappeared, but I know they're behind it. It's almost like they knew that taking the witches would do this to us. Someone has been telling the enemy our secrets. Now I just need to find out theirs so that we can fight back.'

'Agreed.' Cassie couldn't stay awake any longer. She drifted off to sleep without another thought.

Cassie didn't need to open her eyes to know where she was this time. She felt the satin sheets again, and the dim purple color through her barely cracked eyelids let her know she was back in her prisoner room. She had hoped to wake up with Nate—he was all she had left, and she was more than worried about everything. But even she knew that would be a bad choice for the wendigo. They couldn't leave the last two people who were looking for answers together. At least, they still didn't know about the bonding. She could talk to Nate even if she couldn't see him.

'Are you okay?' Cassie asked.

'Yes, no visits from your cousin yet today,' Nate replied.

He still sounded tired. It was going to be a while before he was back up to full strength. At least he was being left alone for now … she hoped. Nate was the kind to keep things like that from her if she would worry. As kids, he never told her anything he thought she would worry about. Old Nate seemed to be around a lot more than Than. Cassie had to take that into account. She momentarily looked through the bond. He seemed weak like he did before she fell asleep, but nothing more had changed.

'Jared came in right after you dozed off. He took you back as quickly as he could,' Nate continued. *'There's something strange about him. Make sure to keep an eye out.'*

Strange was the least of it. Cassie wasn't about to explain the predicament of sleeping in a room that only could be accessed via Jared's bedroom. For some reason, she was quite sure Nate would be irate when he found out.

"Man, you day humans sleep a lot," Ryder remarked, interrupting Cassie's silent conversation.

Cassie sat up, and the air was cold on her arms. She wasn't wearing her long-sleeved shirt from before. Now she was wearing a T-shirt she hadn't put on. She pulled the covers against herself when she noticed it was just a T-shirt and no pants to go with them. She must have been really asleep to not feel someone changing her clothing. Then it hit her. *Who changed my clothing?* Her cheeks reddened.

Ryder stood against the far wall in the room, between the windows filled with fading light. His blond hair almost glowed as the setting sun touched it. He was completely different than his twin brother, and yet she didn't feel the need to put up a protection spell from him. Something was different with him than the first time she met him. She couldn't put her finger on it, but he was different.

He turned back to her like he could feel her assessing him.

"If you want to get dressed, I can give you a tour of this place," he offered. He didn't know what he was even offering her, and Cassie had to hide a grin.

That was a start. Cassie didn't know what to look for, but she was plenty sure that Nate saw the images in her mind just like she could see his. He would need the information of the place to know how to get them out when the time came. Now all he needed to do was recover and then they could leave.

Sliding her legs out of the bed, Cassie noticed she wasn't in chains this time. The chain hung empty from the bedpost.

"You'll have to forgive my brother. He is the better one at following rules. Personally, I wouldn't chain you up." Ryder laughed. "Wouldn't? No, rather I didn't even though he told me to. Where are you going to run off to? We took over the whole city. He's nuts to think you could escape and hide away from us, but then again, this isn't the first time he's been this close to winning you. The other time you were taken away before he even knew what was happening." Ryder ran his hands through his long blond hair.

"I have no idea what you're talking about," Cassie replied. She had met Jared a week ago, and while he was nice, she had no intention of staying or mating with him.

Ryder nodded and continued to stare at Cassie, like he was searching for something.

Cassie kept the blanket over her lap and stared back at him. "And while a tour sounds nice, I kind of don't have anything with me to wear."

Ryder pointed to the doorway next to the one that led downstairs.

"Bathroom and fully stocked closet. I think it's all your size. One thing my brother is very thorough about is planning. Just keep the door cracked open. I don't like following the rules that I think are stupid, like chaining you up, but I do need to keep an eye on you. Until you bond to Jared, it isn't exactly safe around here for you. You smell too delicious to everyone."

Cassie shivered at his last statement. He looked and even somewhat acted different, but his words still scared her. She had seen how much he wanted to feed on her before. She didn't really need to experience that.

"So what you said before about Jared losing me. What did you mean by that?" Cassie inquired loudly from the bathroom, hoping to keep the conversation going so he didn't feel the need to watch her change clothes. "I've never met you guys before last week, and I'm pretty sure I wasn't about to be *won over* by him."

"You really don't remember? I was certain it was a joke. Man, now I owe him twice. First, you have to run to the woods and that cabin, and now you really don't remember us? I'm out a hundred now. This sucks," Ryder complained from his place in the bedroom. He hadn't moved any closer.

She walked into the closet. Ryder was correct; it was fully stocked and better than she would have done herself. First off, she could have never afforded that many clothes, and second, she wouldn't have had the time to organize it all. It must have taken Jared hours just to hang and put everything away—color coordinated and organized perfectly.

"I'm serious," Cassie yelled out to Ryder. "What do you mean by *know you*? I've never met you before."

Cassie snatched a pair of jeans, surprised to find her favorite kind in the right size, and slid into them quickly. She pulled out a T-shirt and sweater next, throwing them on just as quick. She didn't know how long Ryder would leave her alone. Grabbing socks, she made her way back through the bathroom and into the bedroom. She paused by the bed and waited for an answer from him.

Ryder came over to her and looked straight into her eyes. He seemed like he was searching for an answer at first, but then Cassie realized he was giving her an open book. She looked at a memory he was playing in his mind for her. She was young, maybe only five at the time. She was at the park and running around with three boys. When the image cleared, she could tell one was a young Nate. The second boy turned to the one watching everyone play, and she was shocked to find it wasn't Owen like she expected, but someone else. She would recognize those chocolate-brown eyes anywhere. It had to be Jared.

"We grew up with you, even if you can't remember us. My dad said they would erase your memories, but I thought he was just mad. He was mad a lot back then after our mother died. I don't know what changed, but my father joined the wendigo and then so did we. We had no choice. We were forced to leave, and obviously, they stripped everyone of their memories. I didn't think they would actually take yours, and I refused to believe my dad. At first, I thought maybe you didn't recognize us, but then I figured you were just as stuck up as the rest of the coven. Really, I thought you guys were just playing with us. Seems I should say I'm sorry. You're just a pawn in all this also."

Cassie regarded Ryder. He was completely serious even if she didn't have a clue what he was talking about. She tried to will back memories with him in them. There was nothing. She couldn't remember what he looked like as a kid or even having met him. How could he remember, but she couldn't? Were they real memories, or was he just doing it to get her to like them more?

"I have that memory," Cassie finally said as it came to her. "But you and Jared aren't in it. It was of me and Nate playing with Owen. That's when I fell off the slide and thought I broke my arm."

"But Jared convinced you that if you broke your arm, you could never eat ice cream again," Ryder finished the exact memory in his version.

"No, Owen did that. Owen's always done stuff like that," Cassie replied. She could see it clearly, and it was Owen. Ryder was wrong. Maybe he had some sort of spell he was using to try to change her memories. Witches could do that sort of thing; at least, they could in theory. It was against coven rules to do anything mind altering since you could hurt someone as easy as mess with them.

Ryder appeared saddened by Cassie's comment.

"Owen didn't move here until we left the clan eight years ago," Ryder explained.

Cassie shook her head. That memory was almost ten years old. Owen had lived in town their whole lives. He wasn't someone who had moved in. He couldn't have. She had too many memories with him growing up. Owen, Nate, and she were the three besties of all her childhood memories. It was always the three of them together. Always.

"But that does explain a lot. They must have just

overwritten your memories of us and put Owen in their place. No wonder he fit right in." Ryder nodded as he talked.

She could feel that he was certain. He wasn't lying. He had to be mistaken. Maybe his memories were messed with. But then again, maybe hers were. The coven hadn't exactly been nice to her over the years. Could she really still trust them?

"They wouldn't do that," Cassie whispered as her whole childhood came into question. She didn't trust Ryder or the wendigo, but she didn't trust the coven. They had already shown her that they planned to strip her powers.

"I know it doesn't seem true to you, but let me prove it," Ryder suggested, motioning for her to follow him downstairs.

Ryder led the way down into his brother's room. Instead of leaving the room, he turned and walked the opposite direction of the door. He stopped at the well-polished wooden desk. Pulling open drawers, he searched for something. He paused when he pulled out the top drawer and chuckled.

"Of course, he kept it right on top. Here I thought he had hidden it." Ryder removed a folded up piece of paper. "Guess he knew the old man would never look in that obvious of a place."

Ryder handed Cassie the paper and waited for her to open it. Cassie didn't need to open it to know what it was. She recognized it right away. She had written that exact letter for Owen, but never went through giving it to him. She had lost it years ago. It was a letter where she told Owen that she loved him, but they could never be together. They were too close of friends, and she didn't want to ruin that. Even at nine, Cassie knew how the world worked. If she told Owen she liked him and he didn't like her, she would be out her best, and at the time, only friend. She kept all that to herself. She never told anyone about the letter.

"Go ahead and open it." Ryder motioned to the paper.

"I already know what it says. Why does Jared have this? Did you guys stalk me or something? Jared seems to know all sorts of stuff about me," Cassie commented, thinking back to the week before when Jared tried to prove that he knew her. How could someone she never met know that much? They *must* have stalked her.

"Just open it," Ryder replied, not answering yes or no to Cassie's accusations.

'*Dear Jared*' the letter began. Cassie stopped reading and glanced up at Ryder. It was her handwriting, but she was sure it was supposed to say '*Dear Owen*'. It was her letter to Owen, and she didn't even know a Jared when she had written it.

"Is this some sort of trick?" she asked, getting a little more than creeped out. She was left with more questions floating around in her mind.

"Look at the photo if you don't believe us," Ryder added, pointing to the piece of paper that was face down in the letter.

Cassie turned the photo over. It was a picture Cassie had in a frame in her house. She always loved that picture, but never could exactly say why. Owen always laughed at it. He said that he hated how their parents made them all get dressed up for that day, but she never remembered it that way. She remembered a day where she wore a dress, and Uncle John was the kind of man she wished her father would have been. He had taken her to a coven party, and Owen and Nate were her dates. That was the last time the three of them were all friends. But now as she looked at the picture, she wasn't sitting between Owen and Nate. She was sitting and holding onto Nate and someone else completely.

"That was the last time we saw you before the coven kicked us out. Our mother died two weeks before the party. It was really hard on my dad, but everything changed at that party. The seer for the coven met you that day. What we've figured out is that she was supposed to pass the job onto you, but instead she told Mikel you would tear the clan apart since you were fated to be bonded to both Nate and Jared. Mikel immediately kicked us out of the clan and forbade Nate to have anything to do with you." Ryder looked at the picture with Cassie. "I took that picture," he said. "I remember that day exactly. I promise you, this isn't a game. We have known you your whole life. We aren't the monsters everyone says we are."

The old picture was worn at the edges, but it was real. It wasn't a fake and had been well-handled over the years. She looked back at the letter. She could vividly remember writing the letter, but she still couldn't remember it being written to Jared.

"You don't have to believe or trust me, but I'm telling you the truth. You were predicted to bond to both Nate and Jared. They are both your destiny, even if you don't remember that much," Ryder added, taking the picture and letter from Cassie and carefully folding it back up to put it back in its place. "Now how about that tour since you will be here a while? Might as well start finding your way around so I don't have to babysit you."

Cassie nodded and followed him to the door. She gave one last look back to the desk. She couldn't deny it. She felt it, too. Something deep inside told her to trust Jared and that he was safe. How did she know that about someone she just met? It would make a lot more sense that her gut trusted Jared because even if she didn't remember him, part of her did. It was possible and that complicated everything. How many more memories was she forgetting?

The tour took longer than she expected. She thought they were just in a small house from her only trip out of the place, but she was mistaken. The wendigo had made their home in the hills under the cover of the woods surrounding the town, but that didn't mean they were isolated. All of the homes were strategically placed, and it was easy to go from one to the next. Each had a similar layout with bedrooms for the kids to one side of the house, a kitchen and living room in the middle, and the parents' rooms to the other side. There was a large section off the side of the house Ryder said they didn't need to see yet, and Cassie agreed. She got a dark feeling coming from behind the doors. Avoiding it was the best call.

Ryder took her outside to show her the main layout of the community. He told her the names of the people who lived the closest and which pathway led to each one. They all had a house pretty much the same, and all the houses came with a barn. Ryder was vague in his explanation of why they needed barns since it didn't seem like anyone was keeping animals around. In fact, there weren't even any pets.

As they passed the last bend around the property, with Ryder listing who lived down yet another pathway, Cassie felt Nate cut the connection between them, but not quick enough to feel the skin break open across her hand. Ryder froze in his steps. He could smell her blood. Cassie reflexively closed her hand.

"We can go get a bandage in the barn," Ryder suggested.

Cassie froze, looking at the doorway. She knew exactly what was going on behind the door, and she didn't want to see it. If her hand was bleeding, then so was Nate's. And he had cut the connection. Someone was in there with him and draining him of more blood. She figured it wasn't the best idea to go inside, either. Nate broke the connection for a reason.

"Can I just wait out here?" Cassie asked, pointing to a stone wall which lined the driveway.

Ryder glanced around the area. Then he lifted his face into the slight wind. He gave a half shrug.

"You should be safe for just a moment. I'll be right back." Ryder pulled open the door to the barn and disappeared into it.

Cassie nervously took in her surroundings. Her blood attracted night humans, but Ryder seemed to think she was safe. She really didn't trust him, but she found on the tour that he wasn't as scary right now. It kind of even felt like several times that he had turned into a completely different person. Cassie had seen an old movie on TV once where aliens took over the bodies of normal people. If monsters were real, why not aliens?

The woods behind Cassie became unnervingly silent. Cassie couldn't help but feel as her heartbeat picked up. Her intuition was telling her she wasn't alone. The barn wasn't too far away, but Cassie knew by experience that she wasn't faster than the wendigo monsters. She pressed her hand as tightly shut as she could to try to stop her blood from luring them closer. A loud crack sounded behind her. Or maybe it was a small branch breaking. Either way, someone was certainly behind her. Loud breathing moved closer to Cassie. She didn't want to turn around, but she couldn't help it.

At the edge of the woods there stood a large, brown-colored bear. Cassie stared at it, and it stared back. Her mind blanked. What kind of bear was it? Was she supposed to play dead or slowly back away? The one time in her life she finally met a bear, and she forgot what to do.

The bear continued to stand at the tree line and just watch her. It tilted its head like it was studying Cassie and not understanding her reaction. Then it hit her. Was this the same bear she saw the day before? Whitney said it was Uncle John. Could the great big bear before her be her uncle?

Fighting against the feeling that told her to flee from it, Cassie stood and slowly walked toward the bear. He sat down like he was waiting for her. She inched forward more, forcing her body to move against her will. She got two feet away from it and froze. He was even larger up close. The bear looked at Cassie, straight into her eyes.

Instantly images flashed into her mind. Cassie could feel

the anger as her uncle transformed against his will. The whole scene played out before her. The house was surrounded by not only wendigo but a handful of male witches that included a cousin and uncle she had never met. Aunt Maria was yelling at John over all the noise and magic in the air. He laid down for her to climb on and she said a spell. Uncle John didn't wait to see what else the wendigo witches were doing and smashed through the grand picture window at the front of the house. The images fast forwarded, but then abruptly stopped.

'Cassie, I hope you trust John enough to be able to see this. We saw you come home and couldn't get to you before them. They have taken all the witches in town. We don't know yet where they are, but we will find them. They have been tracking me and trying to take me. As long as one witch who belongs to the coven is free, they can't take the town. They won't stop looking for me, but we won't stop searching for everyone else.'

Aunt Maria looked around because the bear in Uncle John could smell magic as it neared. They were still being followed in the memory.

'We will find everyone else; just stay with the wendigo. Do whatever you need to do to survive. And when we find everyone, we will need Nate's help. Tell him that we will find the witches. And also that the clan is intact. The adults who were bonded can't be counted on as they went feral when the connection broke, but we have collected everyone else. Everyone without a mate can talk to John, and he can direct them, just as Nate can if he goes into his animal form. Warn him to be careful. We don't know why they took him and no one else. Stay safe and we will contact you again.'

Cassie blinked, and the bear nodded to her. As strange as it felt, she nodded back. And with that, her uncle was gone, vanishing just as quickly as he came.

She walked back down to where she had been waiting. It had only taken moments to get the message from her aunt, but she wanted to be careful. She didn't want to see Nate or what they were doing to him, yet she was quite certain she needed to tell him what was going on. She needed him to stop blocking her so that she could tell him.

Walking to the barn, Cassie felt someone approaching again. She turned to the woods, expecting to see her uncle. Instead, she saw one of the wendigo they had passed on their tour earlier. Cassie tried to ignore him as a grin appeared on his face.

She felt her body slam into the barn before she registered what was going on.

"What do we have here?" the man asked. He was older than Cassie, probably by only a few years, but it was hard to tell beneath the grime.

He grabbed her arms and pinned them above her head.

"It smells like you have a treat for me." The grubby man's breath smelled putrid blowing against her face.

He grasped her hands with one of his hands while he used his second to unpeel the fingers away from her cut hand. The blood was still dried on it, but at least it was healing over. Cassie watched the man hungrily eye over the cut. He licked his lips, and she didn't have much time to think up her options.

She was close to the barn door. While she didn't want to go into the barn, now it wasn't an option to ignore. Ryder had gone in, and she was pretty sure he was the only one she trusted to keep her safe for the time being. Besides Nate, that is, if Nate weren't bound up to the torture table.

The gross, smelly wendigo man pulled Cassie's arms down to taste her blood. Cassie didn't wait for his tongue to touch her hand as she kicked as hard as she could between the man's legs. He howled in pain and dropped her hands, but not without first grabbing her shoulder as he fell. Cassie felt his claws dig in, and she prepared herself to hit the ground face first. She didn't feel the solid ground because she landed on someone. She felt the wild man's fingers pulled from her shoulder as the world turned fuzzy around her from the pain. She hoped that it didn't mean her uncle returned. She wasn't sure they wouldn't shoot a bear attacking one of their own on sight.

The pain instantly felt relieved, and Cassie squinted to look around her, easing her eyes open from squeezing them shut hard.

Cassie closed her eyes again. There was much more than she wanted to see. From her small glimpse, she was pretty sure that the man would never harass her again. He was in several pieces strewn across the parking lot next to the barn.

"You awake, princess?" Ryder asked from beneath her.

Cassie pushed herself up but kept her eyes closed. She didn't need to see what guts and blood galore looked like again. There had been enough blood when she was attacked a week ago by a wendigo she assumed was Ryder. Now he was busy catching her from hitting the ground and getting hurt further. Again, he was completely confusing her.

"Yes, but I'd prefer to keep my eyes closed for now," Cassie replied. She wasn't going to sneak a second look.

Ryder laughed, and her whole body bounced with each ha.

"A witch without the stomach for blood? You just keep surprising me," Ryder replied, pulling her head to his chest and turning her in the other direction. "That should be fine. You can open your eyes that way."

Ryder was more than gentle with her as he moved her around. Was he even the same person she met the week before?

"Can I look at where he cut you?" Ryder asked.

Slowly, Cassie opened her eyes. He had angled her perfectly so that she wouldn't see a bit of blood or more. She turned to Ryder, and he moved to block her view.

"I don't smell fresh blood, but we need to be sure it's not open. It isn't like we have too much in the way of medical supplies access around here, but I'm sure we can take you to town if we need an antibiotic," Ryder continued to explain. He pulled on the neck of her shirt to look at her shoulder where the claws of the monster went into her.

"I think I'm fine," Cassie finally replied. Ryder gave her a look that said he didn't really believe her. "Seriously. I'm guessing the mate-bond thingy with Nate absorbed it all."

Ryder still didn't seem convinced. Cassie tugged on the neck of her shirt a little bit to expose where the guy's nails went into her. Under crusted blood, which she had to rub away, it was healed to the point of just being a red mark. Ryder brushed more of the dried blood off her and shook his head.

"Jack said your mating bond would heal you both, but I figured he was lying. I've seen what he's been doing to Nate, and you look fine," Ryder replied, sliding Cassie's shirt back in place once he was convinced she was fine. "Guess I owe Jack five dollars."

"Do you guys bet on everything?" Cassie patted her shirt to be sure it was in place.

Ryder shrugged. "I guess. How is it you aren't walking around looking like a chopping board?"

"Nate severs the mating bond between us until he heals so that I'm not all cut up. Maybe you guys could just quit doing that to him, and life would be easier," Cassie scolded Ryder.

He laughed. "And if we did, your life might be easier, but ours wouldn't. You don't have the slightest clue who you picked for a mate, do you? You've been like this forever. Even as a kid, you never understood any of the politics. They've always just been Nate and Jared to you."

Cassie stared at Ryder. What was he not saying?

"How about you keep your hands off my future mate," Jared growled as he came up behind Cassie. She moved to turn, but Ryder was quicker and stopped her.

"I'd do that, but you made a mess of the place. She's a bit queasy. Can you believe that? A witch that doesn't like blood. Isn't that funny?" Ryder kept his arm around Cassie to keep her from turning.

Jared reached down and picked Cassie up into his arms like she weighed nothing. "Keep your eyes closed and I'll tell you when we're past all of this."

Cassie squeezed her eyes shut. The first time was bad enough, but it seemed like Jared planned to walk through all of it again. Cassie kept her face buried in his chest. He had just a thin shirt on, and he smelled like lemons and soap now.

"Sorry, that took a few minutes. I had to change and get clean before I came back for you," Jared explained the scents clinging to him.

"By the way, bro, clean this all up," Jared called over his shoulder.

"But I didn't make the mess," Ryder complained.

Jared didn't even stop walking as he replied, "And I wouldn't have had to make the mess if you did your job of keeping Cassie safe. It's kind of your fault."

CHAPTER 5

Jared abruptly dropped Cassie when he stepped into his bedroom. Safe now that she was away from everything, Cassie opened her eyes. Jared wasn't even looking at her. He was staring at the staircase leading to her tower room, and he wasn't happy.

"We have a guest. Or rather, you have a guest." Jared nodded upstairs, not even moving toward them.

"Uninvited?" Cassie asked, slightly scared to go anywhere without Jared. It was clear that even if she pretended she was safe with the wendigo that was very far from the case. Jared was the only one who seemed to care if she were safe.

"Invited? Never, but you don't have to be afraid." Jared had to have noticed her heart rate pick up. "Can I see where he cut you?" Jared pointed to her shoulder, choosing to ignore their guest.

Cassie pulled at her collar again, but this time, she was a bit shy and had no idea why. Jared wasn't much different than his brother, yet he was. There was something she couldn't put her finger on. Maybe it was the way he looked at her with genuine concern in his eyes, or maybe it was how he softly touched the marks that were almost gone. Jared was different than the rest of the wendigo.

"Does it hurt at all?" he asked.

"No. It's all healed over." It was close to one-hundred-percent normal. It hurt when it happened, but not now.

"Then we better get up to your guest before he comes down here."

"My guest?" Cassie was now confused. Were there more wendigo she didn't remember?

Jared motioned for her to go upstairs. She glanced back behind her, and he nodded in encouragement. Cassie had the feeling Jared would never let her go somewhere unsafe, but she was still cautious. Step by step she climbed to the bedroom, her heart beating faster and faster. Cassie paused at the top of the stairs and just stared at the guy sitting on her bed.

Nate noticed Cassie and instantly jumped up and grabbed her, crushing her to him.

"What the hell happened?" he grumbled, his words muffled by his arm around her.

"You might want to let go if you want her to be able to breathe," Jared suggested as he came to the top step.

Nate set Cassie down and jumped across the room in an instant. Jared vanished as quickly as Nate moved, but it didn't seem to matter. Nate anticipated his movements and shifted with him. As Nate pulled back to slug Jared, Jared vanished and appeared beside Cassie. They bounced around the room with Nate trying to attack Jared. He was getting closer with each swing.

Cassie finally got control of her shock. They were both moving faster than seemed physically possible. Neither of them was human, but it was never more evident than in that exact moment.

"Stop!" Cassie demanded, moving between them in her snail-like pace compared to the guys.

Nate paused at her voice and froze mid-step.

"And why shouldn't I beat the crap out of him? Here I'm playing nicely and letting them drain my blood day after day only so that he can let you get fed upon by one of his kind?" Nate was fuming, but amazingly keeping everything under control.

"I didn't let anyone do that to Cassie. I was with my father," Jared replied. "Ryder was supposed to be watching her." Even Jared was mad about the situation.

"Obviously not watching since he was more than happy to help out Jack." Nate glared at Jared.

"He will be dealt with later," Jared replied. "Now that you see she's okay, you can go back to your cage and sit there like a good little puppy." Jared waved his hands like he was dismissing Nate.

Nate moved to jump at Jared again, but Cassie put her arm on him before he moved. He stopped in his tracks.

"I'm fine. Really," Cassie tried to calm him down. She could feel through the bond that he was a mixture of anger and relief after being scared for her.

"If I hadn't heard you, though …" Nate looked like what happened pained him more than her.

"It's fine. Everything is taken care of," Cassie told him, reaching up to touch the wound she had received which had obviously transferred to him. It was healing much slower on him.

Nate caught her hand and held onto it.

"Until we get this all straightened out, I'm not leaving your side." Nate stared into her eyes as he made his promise.

"Um … don't you have to go back to being a prisoner? I get the feeling they wouldn't be keen on you walking around."

Nate glanced over her shoulder at Jared.

"Since you've proven you can't protect her at all times, I'm staying right here with Cassie." He talked like he was in charge even though they were completely at the mercy of the wendigo.

Jared leaned against the doorway as he watched them, and when she met his gaze, he shrugged. It was almost like he was just as used to Nate's bossy attitude as Cassie was. He wasn't fighting it, but he didn't completely agree, either.

"What makes you so much more qualified to protect her? Out of your night human form you are almost as weak as a day human. You can't even catch me," Jared taunted him.

Cassie felt Nate's anger flare across the bond. He was going to lose it and outright attack Jared, which wouldn't do well for Cassie. She was already exhausted from just moments before. Cassie grasped Nate's hand tighter to keep him from moving.

"I protect her because she's mine," Nate said through gritted teeth. "If I hadn't heard what was going on and opened the bond back up, she would have died from blood loss. What would you have done then? I'm the only one who can protect her at all times."

"Things never change, do they?" Jared muttered. Cassie was unsure if it was said to himself or Nate. "Do you really think you're special because she chose you? She came to us to try to break the mating bond you forced on her. There's nothing special about that."

"She chose me," Nate replied, puffing out his chest.

"Chose you? You merely kissed her first," Jared responded.

"She still chose me," Nate answered, undeterred by Jared's response.

"If you're sure, let me demonstrate something for you."

Jared walked cautiously closer. He held out his hand for Cassie. She looked to Nate, but he seemed as confused as she was. Cassie carefully took Jared's hand, letting go of Nate and hoping he could control his urge to continue fighting with Jared. She didn't want to be caught in the middle of them.

Leaning forward, Jared pressed his lips to Cassie's. Something clicked in Cassie's mind, and it felt right—perfect—like she had been waiting a lifetime to kiss him even though she just met him. It was strange. She wanted to pull back and try to understand where all the feelings were coming from, but she couldn't. She was frozen with her lips to his.

Cassie's heart beat uncontrollably. It wasn't her first kiss ever, Nate had taken that, but it felt like her first time ever kissing someone.

Jared pulled back so that their noses were still touching.

"I've been waiting long enough to do that," he said, his voice rough and his eyes an open book for Cassie to read. She was still confused, but her body wasn't. She felt like she had known him her whole life and had been waiting for that kiss.

The burn around her wrist caused her to break his gaze and not look into his memories. It was exactly the same as when it happened on her neck when she didn't know that Nate had claimed her as his mate. Those lines were still there according to everyone that could see them, but now she was certain there were new ones. She didn't need to see them to know they were there. When the burning stopped, it finally hit her. Years of memories flooded into her mind. Cassie dropped to her knees as the weight of everything came back to her. Nate grabbed one elbow and Jared the other as they jointly ushered her to the bed.

"Cassie, are you okay?" Nate asked, rubbing the new invisible mark on her hand.

Cassie tried to look at Nate, but her eyes grew unfocused as the memories continued to come back. She closed her eyes instead. It was an information overload.

"What's happening?" Nate growled at Jared, seeing Cassie in pain.

"Beats me. You're the one that's done this choosing a mate thing before. This was my first time," Jared replied rather snarkily.

"Stop arguing," Cassie told them. Her head was pounding from all the new information.

'Cassie, are you okay?' Nate asked silently, half with concern, and half-testing that the bond was still there.

'Yes. Just a lot to process,' Cassie replied, flopping back on the bed with her eyes still closed.

'Process? Was this the same as when I bonded to you?'

'No. This isn't about that. I remember now.' Cassie

rubbed her head.

'Remember what?'

Cassie suddenly remembered Nate had been left out of all that had happened since she last saw him the day before. She sat up but her head spun, and she had to lie back down.

'We need to talk, like soon.' Cassie peeked out from beneath her eyelashes to see both Nate and Jared staring at her with concern.

'Give me something or I won't be responsible if I go all animal-like on everyone,' Nate replied, still filled with concern.

'Shortened version: We all knew Jared and his family when we were kids. We grew up together, and the coven changed our memories to make us think it was Owen, not Jared.'

'Impossible,' Nate interrupted her.

'Let me finish before Jared gets pissed and figures out we can talk this way,' Cassie continued as quickly as she could, still lying on the bed like her head was her only problem. *'I saw my uncle when I was waiting for Ryder. Maria sent me a message that they are looking for the witches and that all the younger skinwalkers without a mate can still talk with you. Only the older ones who were mated went feral when the witches were taken. In your animal form, you can talk to everyone, including John since he doesn't have a mate. Maria didn't come because the wendigo are still looking for her, and as long as she's around, they can't take the town from the witches.'*

Cassie carefully sat up again, still rubbing her head.

She slowly looked Jared over. He was just as she had pictured teen him to be when she was a kid, but she could still see the boy they spent hours with. He waited with his face full of concern.

"I wouldn't have done that if I knew it was going to hurt you," Jared explained.

"I know," Cassie replied shyly. She remembered Jared

completely, but it had been almost eight years since she last saw him. He was as much stranger as he was a friend. He was a mixture. "You've always protected me mentally where Nate was the one to protect me physically."

Jared sucked in his breath. "You remember," he said quietly.

"Everything," Cassie replied, staring up into his honey-amber eyes. There was much swirling around in her thoughts, but he was still Jared. She knew him. He was really her best friend, not Owen. Every single childhood memory she thought was with Owen, was really Jared.

"Shoot," Jared exclaimed, jumping up from the bed. "Both of you stay up here. I'll be right back."

He disappeared downstairs before there was a knock at his door. Cassie took a deep breath. Things had just gotten way more complicated. It was easy to believe Ryder was delusional about her past, and actually, she wanted it to be that, but it made sense. Jared had the letter and even a picture of her and Nate. He knew much about her because he actually knew her. He could counter and fight with Nate, because he knew Nate. They all had grown up together. So why was Jared a wendigo and Nate a skinwalker? For every one answer, Cassie now had two questions.

Nate stood by the stairway and listened to the conversation happening in the room below. Cassie wanted to talk more with him, but she was sure what they needed to talk about had to be a silent conversation. Since his concentration seemed to be on the room beneath them, Cassie didn't want to interrupt him.

Cassie could only hear muffled talk from below, but that didn't seem to be the same for Nate. The door to the room opened and shut, and Nate hurried over to the window. He watched outside for a few minutes before finally turning back to her.

"What's up?" she asked, hating that she was left in the dark again.

"Jack just stopped by. He was freaking out about me being loose and something about not being able to skin me," Nate replied, still staring out the window.

Cassie shivered. Her cousin seemed a bit on the bad side and all, but skinning Nate? That sounded beyond a "bit" bad. His torture seemed to be escalating, which was horrible.

"Jared never said I was up here," Nate added, more perplexed than Cassie was.

She had the memories of their past. Jared might be a wendigo and on the other side, but he wasn't a bad guy. He never was. She didn't know him from the past years, but when she looked into his eyes, she could see it. That part of him would never change. He was always going to be a good guy. It was just part of him.

"Why'd they leave?" Cassie asked, not sure who Nate was watching more, Jared or Jack as they walked outside.

"To get a kit for you to do magic. Jack was a bit upset that Jared would want that as he doesn't trust you to be on their side, but Jared assured him that you were already marked as his mate. I can't tell who's in charge, but it seemed like Jared has more power than Jack." Nate stood, but still watched outside.

"How could Jared have grown up with us if he's a wendigo?"

Nate finally turned from the window. "Whitney said she was going to explain all of this to you, but I'm figuring she left out a few details."

"Like …"

"Like the wendigo are made from the skinwalkers," Nate replied.

"Made from?"

"When a skinwalker goes bad, they become a wendigo. When I said we were the good guys, I literally meant the good guys. If you do a deed that is so bad it taints your soul, you lose your animal and become one of them. A creature stuck, unable to change into what you are naturally."

Cassie sucked in her breath. She hadn't seen Jared, but she was pretty sure that he was a wendigo. Did that mean he was bad?

"So what you're saying," Cassie paused so that she could word it correctly, "is the wendigo are skinwalkers?"

"They were, or their parents or a long-lost relative were at one time. Once they become a wendigo, they can't go back to being a skinwalker. They curse their whole family." Nate walked back over to the window.

Cassie watched him silently as he thought. His mannerisms showed that he was as worried and as confused as she was, but she didn't want to pry too much. He didn't have the same memories as she did. He wanted to believe her memories, but his own mind still had Owen in place of Jared. Luckily for Cassie, Nate believed her over the coven and trusted her for now.

The door to Jared's room opened and closed again. Jared made his way upstairs, and Nate moved to step between them. Jared stopped in the doorway and held his hand up.

"Whoa, kitty. I'm not about to do anything that would hurt her. She's my mate now, too," Jared replied.

Cassie rubbed her hand where she knew the invisible mark was. Nate looked down at her hand and finally noticed it.

"Impossible," he muttered, taking her hand in his.

It has to be a night human thing to see the bond mark, Cassie concluded.

"How can we get his memories back?" Cassie asked as Nate stared at her hand.

She needed him to remember. She now knew it wasn't impossible for her to have two mates. In fact, Jack was more than right that she could bind to as many night humans as she wanted. She needed to know why Jack knew this, and what it meant.

"Yours came back when I kissed you," Jared replied.

Nate glared at Jared. "Not about to happen, buddy."

Cassie rolled her eyes. Jared had to see the truth even if Nate didn't. They had been friends and knew just how to push each other's buttons.

"Mine came back when your mark showed up," Cassie explained, trying to get off the kissing part because it was still too confusing.

"Still not going to happen for us," Nate replied, glaring at Jared before he could suggest it.

"I don't know how to get the memories back for him. I didn't know binding to you would do it for you. They don't exactly tell you how to unscrew up your life when they throw you out of the clan," Jared replied. "But I'll suggest that you turn into your animal soon before Jack traces you here. He's dead set on skinning your animal from you."

Nate continued to glare at Jared. It was obvious he didn't trust him a single bit, and he was a little perplexed by him offering to help.

"I get it. You skinwalker, me enemy wendigo," Jared said in a mock caveman voice. "We hate all."

Now Nate was more confused. Jared wasn't just trying to help him, but was making fun of the whole situation.

Cassie raised her hand since neither guy seemed to notice her. Jared smiled as he turned to her.

"Um, can you explain what skinning Nate entails? Because I might suggest he run far away from here, not just turn into his tiger."

Nate didn't seem to agree with that suggestion, but he was just as curious.

Jared shook his head. "Sometimes I forget how unfair this is to you guys. You don't have all the same cards as us. Man, if I were you, I'd be pissed at your father. He did this to you guys."

Nate lifted his head and closed his eyes, sensing the world around him. "Let's get back to the skinning part because Jack should be here in about two minutes."

"Skinning you. It's a term we use to mean stripping your animal. There is all this magic stuff of catching you as you shift that allows us to take your animal from you," Jared spat out.

Cassie's eyes got big, and Nate's anger flared.

"You were going to turn me into one of you?" He pointed his finger at Jared.

"Me? No. I don't want you as a wendigo. It would majorly suck. Jack? Well, he does. He seems to think if we turn you, then it will break your father, and the whole clan will fall. I don't think it's that easy. And I don't want you as one of us," Jared replied.

There was a knock on the door again.

"Your choice, man. Be your tiger and stay safe, or go back to being Jack's new toy." Jared turned and went back downstairs.

"Do you trust him?" Nate asked. Jared was obviously taking his time going down the stairs and making his way to the doorway.

"Yes," Cassie whispered. Logically Jared had to be evil to be one of them since Cassie could remember he was once a skinwalker, but Cassie's heart said otherwise. The Jared she remembered could never be evil.

Nate stood up and pulled Cassie into his arms. He kissed her almost as quickly as their first kiss before stepping back and changing into his tiger, his clothing shredding as the large black and orange beast appeared.

Tiger Nate moved in front of Cassie and waited. Cassie heard Jared talking to Jack as they climbed the stairs. Jack got upstairs first, and his face fell. Jared had been right. He obviously had been trying to catch Nate in his day human form and was now severely disappointed.

"I told you if Nate was here, he wouldn't sit around as a human," Jared added.

"He's no use to me now." Jack turned and left the way he

came without a word to Cassie or Nate.

'Are you going to turn back?' Cassie asked.

'Not a chance. Looks like Jared was right. Jack did have plans for me. I thought he was trying to make me change before. This just confirms it. And Jared was also right that I'm better at defending you in this form. Why does he have to be right?' A glimpse of Nate's time with Jack shone through his mind to Cassie. She shivered at the image of Nate being cut repeatedly to take his blood.

'He knows us, and I don't think he's the evil you guys say the wendigo are. We just need to figure out what it means. We were all friends once. Why did the coven get rid of his family?'

After shutting the door downstairs, Jared returned to Cassie and Nate.

"He's not about to give up. He really thinks making you a wendigo is the answer to everything." Jared shrugged. "For my sake, please just stay a tiger."

'My dad would never break just because I was gone. He doesn't care that much,' Nate told Cassie.

She doubted that. All of her memories from her childhood told her that Nate's dad cared, and cared a lot. Jack might have been closer to the truth than Nate realized.

"You can turn someone into a wendigo from taking their animal?" Cassie asked.

She had all sorts of new memories, but anything clan specific wasn't really taught to her. She was only a kid and not yet into studies at school when Jared left. After that, everything was kept from her.

"We have two kinds of wendigo. The first level is someone who comes from the wendigo line or is forced to be one. We call that a pledge level. That's the kind you've met already. All the younger people around here are still pledges." Jared shook his head.

Cassie looked at him as he gave a grim laugh.

"Okay, it sounds even stranger explaining it out loud. It

makes it sound like we have a choice in the matter. Pledge. What a joke." Jared turned to leave.

"And the second level?" Cassie asked.

Jared glanced back over his shoulder. "Hope you never meet one of those."

A shiver ran down Cassie's spine. The pledge wendigo were bad enough. She really didn't need to be told that the full members would be worse. She could have guessed that much.

"If you want to set up spells around the rooms, it might make you both feel a bit safer," Jared suggested.

"How would I?"

"I went with Jack to grab a stocked witch kit. It's downstairs. It should have everything basic and maybe a bit more in it. I know you witches like to use your own stuff, but your uncle didn't leave your house in the best condition. I'm not sure there's much left there to scavenge."

With that, Jared left the room. Cassie turned back to Nate. His big tiger eyes looked at her once he was sure Jared was downstairs.

'He's right. It would be better for you to put spells around the room to keep us safe. I can't stay awake forever because I'm too low on blood,' Nate stated.

Cassie followed Jared downstairs. Staying at the top of the stairs, Nate looked down into the room.

"With what you've been doing to Nate, won't being low on blood keep him from protecting me?" Cassie asked.

Jared looked up at the stairway and sighed. Walking over to the mini fridge under his desk, Jared took out hospital bags of blood.

"It's donated blood," Jared explained as Cassie stared at the bags in his hands. "I get it from the hospital because I refuse to hunt humans like everyone else around here."

'It will do,' Nate told Cassie.

"I'll feed him and then set up the wards," Cassie explained, reaching for the bags. Whether it grossed her out or not, this was her world now. She was part of it, and it was high time to suck it up and deal with it.

Jared shook his head. "I got that. I'll get him the blood, and you get everything set up. I have a feeling it won't be safe around here until you do."

Turning, Cassie glanced at Nate. He nodded his tiger head, like he agreed even though he could speak to her in her mind.

"Where is the kit?" Cassie asked as Jared walked up the stairs.

"By the door," Jared replied.

Moving toward the door, she saw that there were several bags thrown against the wall, like they had been dropped by Jared as he came into the room. Cassie turned back to ask which one, but Jared was already upstairs. When she walked to the stairway to ask Jared, she heard him talking to Nate.

"You better not make me regret this," Jared was saying. "And you better never tell my father about this. He would kill me for it. I'm only doing this because I need your help keeping her safe. I won't be full strength until I bond with her, and until then there are many that can hurt her."

Cassie hurried back to the door at the mention of people around to hurt her. She needed to do her part. She reached down and took the closest duffle bag, hoping that since it was closest, it was the most recently dropped by the door. She was rewarded when she looked inside. It was filled with plastic boxes of herbs. Needing a large space to set them all out, Cassie took in her surroundings. The desk, while clean and neatly organized, wasn't enough room. There was a coffee table with a bit more room, but Cassie really needed more. Finally, she realized the only place with enough space was Jared's well-made bed. She started to haul the bag over to his bed, but it was heavier than she expected. Jared was instantly beside her, picking it up for her.

"Where do you want it?" he asked, lifting it like it weighed nothing.

Night humans. To him, it probably did weigh nothing.

"I was going to use your bed to spread it all out and see what's in there," Cassie answered.

"Sounds good," Jared replied as he moved the bag for her. Cassie followed him to his bed. "If you need anything else, I can go get it. Jack is always well set with everything, and he lives just down the hill."

Cassie hoped Nate heard that. It, at least, gave them a better sense as to where they were. They still couldn't leave as they had nothing to go back to, but it was good to know.

The bag was filled, and Cassie began to take out box after box. It wasn't hard to find what she needed with the nicely labeled boxes.

"This is a nice stash," Cassie commented, putting back the plants she didn't need.

Jared shrugged.

'Staying upstairs?' Cassie asked Nate, expecting to see him behind Jared.

'For now. I was tired before I was fed. Now I'm just exhausted. Don't leave the room without me, and if anything seems even a little off, scream at me through the bond. I'll be there in the blink of an eye.'

Cassie watched Jared, who was picking the full bag back up to move it next to the door. She could feel she was safe with him, but it was nice Nate felt that way also. She remembered Jared even if Nate didn't. He had been their friend once.

The boxes were all set out nicely, and Jared even handed Cassie a bowl to start prepping the potion to use to keep the room safe. Cassie began picking the plants and adding them in the right order.

"You remember everything now?" Jared asked cautiously as he watched her make her potion.

"I remember you," Cassie replied, not exactly knowing what *everything* he was talking about. "But it's weird. It's like I have two sets of every memory now. The ones with you and Ryder, and then the ones with Owen. I know the Owen ones aren't real, and they feel more dreamlike now, but it's still strange."

She continued to work. It was a quick potion to make, but she wanted to be sure it was perfect. She understood better now. Her life pretty much depended on it. Ryder said she smelled tasty, but that seemed to be an understatement. And Jared's comment about how he didn't feed on humans like everyone else had Cassie a bit on edge.

"I'm sorry about that. I always wondered why you never came looking for me. I was angry at you for quite some time. We were best friends." Jared sounded hurt, and Cassie could even slightly feel it across the new bond she had with him. It wasn't as strong as her full bond with Nate, but it was still there.

Cassie nodded as she finished adding the last ingredient. When Jared held out his hand to take it from her to crush, Cassie chuckled. She could remember pretending to do spells as a kid and Jared doing the exact same thing. It was like he knew what she was thinking. Cassie handed it over, and Jared began to pulverize the herbs much easier than it would be for her.

"It's strange to discover that every memory of my childhood was a fake."

After continuing to mush it for a few minutes, he was done and handed it back to Cassie. Taking the bottle of water sitting on his desk, she added it to the paste, then reached down and swiped a little bit onto her pinkie. She tasted it and couldn't help but scrunch up her face. Protection spells were always bitter.

Cassie walked over to the doorway and began to anoint it with the spell. Sitting on the futon, Jared watched her silently as she worked. When she was satisfied the room was safe, she put the leftovers on his desk and sat down beside him.

Jared was still the boy she remembered, and she could

very much see it in him. The dimple that she always loved was still there. His hair, while longer than she had ever seen it growing up, was still the same chestnut brown. His eyes were still the same honey brown that matched hers. He was still the same guy, but it had been almost eight years. Eight years was a long time, and things had changed. Cassie had changed. She wasn't the same happy-go-lucky child she was back then. It had been hard being an outcast and never knowing why.

Cassie tucked her legs up beneath her to keep warm, and Jared immediately jumped up to grab her a blanket.

"How do you know me that well? When I look at you, it's like we're a lifetime apart."

Jared sat back down, but this time closer.

"I've never stopped thinking of you and sneaking into town on occasion to watch you," Jared admitted, his face turning a little red. "I made sure no one ever caught me, wendigo or skinwalker, but I had to see you from time to time."

"What happened to you when they took away my memories?" Cassie asked, changing the subject as it didn't just embarrass Jared, but made her stomach flutter a bit in a way she didn't want it to. It was bad enough she had feelings for Nate when she didn't want them, Jared too was too much.

"Do you remember our last day together, the three of us at the harvest celebration?" Jared asked.

Cassie remembered that day well now. She'd been led to believe she was always an outcast from the town, but it turned out that was just the last eight years. The first eight years, Cassie was being raised by John and Maria with the support of the town. She was accepted, and no one feared her.

"The three musketeers," Cassie laughed. John would call them that often—Cassie, Jared, and Nate were inseparable.

"We were excited we were finally old enough to go to the

celebration," Jared added. "We played all the games and went to all the booths. It was so much fun."

Remembering it, Cassie smiled. It had been a cool fall night. The lanterns were lit around town and each store had a booth outside. There were games and prizes. Nate won the pie eating contest while Jared won the blindfolded race. She could remember cheering for each of them as they competed.

The last booth they stopped at was someone dressed as an old lady. They laughed as she said she would tell them their future. It was supposed to be a silly booth. None of the kids knew it was real. None of them knew everything was going to change by touching the lady. Cassie looked up at Jared. The memories came back fast. She remembered running home and writing the note. Something had happened even if she didn't know how or when.

"You brought me the note, and I never saw you again," Jared stated. He still had the letter she wrote.

Cassie shivered, this time not because she was cold.

Jared moved closer and took Cassie's hands in his own. "What did you see?"

Cassie couldn't say it out loud. That would make it real even if there was no chance of it happening now.

"It was just a silly game that we should never have played," Cassie added. The old lady had set up a table, and they were asked to pull something that called to them from the pile of stuff. When Cassie picked Jared's piece, she had a glimpse of the future, or *a* future. Even now she couldn't be sure how she did it. Cassie was used to seeing the past or people's feelings, but since that day, or even before that day, Cassie had never seen the future.

"Cas, what did you see?"

Cassie shook her head as a tear dribbled down her cheek. She wasn't going to say the words out loud. It was never going to come true. She finally had her friend back, not matter what he was. Jared wasn't going to die.

Reaching up, Jared brushed the tear from her cheek. Then

he moved close enough that he was just inches from her face.

"I know you saw something bad, but that's in the past. This is different now. Everything has changed," he tried to reassure her, even though he didn't know what was wrong.

It was very "Jared" of him. One of her main childhood memories was that Jared always tried to protect her heart. He wasn't as strong as Nate, but he was better at the nice stuff. She never once thought of them in competition. It would be like comparing apples with oranges. While Nate was great at some things and Jared not, Jared was good at others while Nate was not. They complemented each other.

As a little girl growing up, everyone teased her that she had both Jared and Nate as best friends. They always told her that when she was a teenager, it was going to stink because she was going to have to choose. She could only have one of them as her mate. Now she had both. But that didn't mean she was going to keep them both. She had to hope everything was different. It sure wasn't what she had seen, but her gut told her otherwise. Jared and Nate were always set up to be sworn enemies. The truce they had now was only to protect her. That would change as soon as she was safe. She had a feeling neither one was going to accept her not choosing anyone. She was still stuck.

CHAPTER 6

Jared stood to answer the door when someone knocked, but couldn't get the door to open at first. Cassie smiled. The spell was working great. Jared chuckled as the spell released, and he finally managed to open the door.

"Hey, what's going on?" Ryder complained, stepping forward but running into the ward that kept the room safe.

"Guess you're a threat to someone in the room. Spell's working perfect," Jared turned and gave Cassie a thumbs-up. He was enjoying his brother being locked out by the magic.

Cassie smiled back at Ryder and Jared.

"Hey, I'm not a threat," he complained, rubbing his face. "I really thought you were safe. I would have never left you out there alone if I thought someone was stupid enough to attack you."

Cassie knew he was telling the truth. She remembered Ryder as well as Jared, even if he hung out with different people. The Ryder she remembered wasn't a bad person, but she wasn't sure he was the same even if Jared claimed they were still as they once were. Cassie had seen a much darker side to Ryder, one that said he needed to stay on the opposite side of the barrier.

"What's going on?" Jared asked, trying to hurry his brother along.

"Jack lost Nate. Dad's calling, and I have to go report. What should I tell him?" Ryder seemed a bit worried.

Cassie could vaguely remember their father and wondered why Ryder was worried.

"I have Nate here. He's fine and won't be going

anywhere without Cassie. Since Cassie is now my mate, I don't think we have any problems," Jared replied.

Cassie held up her hand for Ryder to see the invisible mark. She didn't want Jared as a mate, but it was keeping Nate safe as he recovered.

"Oh," Ryder replied as he stared at Cassie in shock. "Guess there isn't anything else to talk about."

Jared nodded and shut the door. Returning to the futon, he sat next to Cassie.

"What happened to you guys?" she asked, hoping Jared would stay off the subject of their last day together as kids.

Jared averted his gaze. Now it was a memory he didn't want to share.

"They wanted to kick us out, but didn't know how. My dad was always loyal to the clan, and my mother was part of the coven. They decided to send her off on a peace mission that wasn't exactly peaceful."

Cassie could remember his mother. She looked a lot like Jared with dark hair and dark eyes. She was always baking cookies. Cassie could almost remember the smell of their house better than what it looked like. She was a great cook.

"Where is she? I'd love to see her again," Cassie commented.

Jared glanced down at the floor before taking a breath and looking back at Cassie.

"The coven set her up to be killed. She never returned from the mission. All we got back were her bloodied clothing and her wedding ring."

Jared's words sparked a hidden memory. Cassie could remember his mother going missing. It was heartbreaking for everyone, but it was different for Jared. He was such a stoic child. Cassie wondered if by always protecting her heart that he left his vulnerable.

"It tore my dad apart. He was inconsolable," Jared continued. "He felt her across the bond on the mission. She was scared and worried. She was sad and in pain, and then it broke. The bond ended when she died, and it broke my father. He was never the same, and knew that the coven had sent her away to die. He swore he'd never support the coven ever again and turned to the wendigo. He volunteered to join them and had his animal stripped from him."

Cassie didn't know how to respond. No one's ever said anything about Jared or his family since, and no one had said a witch had died. She would have remembered that. Again, something was altered in her mind, or maybe in the minds of everyone.

"And you? How did you join them?" Cassie asked. Jared was a skinwalker. It was something that was as part of him as she was a witch. It wasn't something you just gave up.

"Has Nate told you about blood connections yet?" Jared asked, changing the subject.

"Like the bond stuff Whitney explained?" Cassie had to tread lightly. She wasn't sure what Jared suspected.

"No, not bonding. It's a way to talk and share images with someone without the bond," Jared explained.

Cassie appeared doubtful at him.

"If I cut my hand and you cut yours, we can press the wounds together and the blood that touches can allow us to communicate while we are touching for that moment," Jared explained further.

"Wouldn't that bond you together? Don't you just have to exchange blood to be bonded?" Cassie asked suspiciously.

Jared laughed. "I can't imagine what all of this is like for you. When we were kids, you were being raised just like us. You understood all of this. It feels like you are still the Cassie I left behind eight years ago, like nothing changed, but at the same time, nothing was taught to you over those eight years."

"Nothing was taught to me," Cassie replied. "Okay, maybe not *nothing*. I learned all about magic and spells, but nothing about this world." Cassie flapped her hands around, indicating the room and everything else around her that was *this world.*

"I'm sorry. I shouldn't laugh. I'm willing to teach you anything you want to know about *this world.*" Jared mimicked her and flapped his arms.

Cassie smiled at him doing it.

"This blood connection doesn't bind you to someone?" Cassie asked, getting back on the subject.

"No. That has to do with ingesting blood, not just touching. Touching can create a connection to temporarily share."

Cassie stared at Jared, trying to weigh what he was saying. Since she was bonded to Nate, she theoretically couldn't bind to someone else. But then again, she should have been only able to have one mate, and that didn't seem to be the case now.

"Cas, I want more than anything to be bonded to you, but I would never trick you into something like unnamed people did to you." Jared looked straight into her eyes. He was being completely honest and open with her. "I want you to bond to me. That's what I want. No tricks. I promise."

"If I cut myself, Nate's going to know and come right down here," Cassie added as Jared reached for a knife from inside his desk drawer next to the pencils.

"He won't even know," Jared replied. "He hasn't been fed for long enough; I doubt he will wake unless you're in a dire panic. Let's say it's a bit like Thanksgiving for him. Four pints of blood is enough to knock out young night humans at least for a few hours."

Cassie gave him her best stare that said *are you pulling my leg?* Jared laughed again.

"You didn't drug him, did you?"

"Cas, he is safe; you are safe. I promise everything's fine right now. You wanted to know what happened, and there's no way I can put it into words. If you want to see, then let me show you. As long as you promise to show me about that day you gave me the good-bye letter."

Cassie sucked in her breath. She thought they had moved on from that subject. Obviously, Jared had not. Cassie weighed her options. She really wanted to know what happened and how he became one of the wendigo, and it seemed he wanted to know why she wrote the letter. Things were different. They couldn't end the same. Too much had changed. Maybe there was no harm in showing him as long as she didn't say the words. Then it wouldn't come true. At least, she hoped. She still didn't understand her powers or what they meant.

"But I get to cut my own hand," she said, taking the knife from him.

Jared shook his head. "Always in charge, just like old times. You do realize Nate and I never did anything that you didn't say was okay, right?"

"Sure you did. There was tons of stuff you guys did that I said would get you in trouble, and it did every time." Cassie held the blade over her finger. *What's one more cut?*

"Sure, we got into trouble. What kid doesn't? But we never did something if you told us not to."

Cassie poked the tip of her finger.

"Is that enough?" she asked.

Jared took the blade from her. After slicing the palm of his hand, he grasped her bleeding finger in his hand.

"And what do we do now? Some sort of chant or something?" Cassie asked as nothing seemed to happen.

'Nope. No chanting needed. Just thoughts,' Jared replied.

Cassie smiled. *'You first.'*

She still didn't know about sharing everything with him, but if he was honest with her, then she would be with him. He deserved the truth. He and Nate had been her best friends. She would have never written the letter if she had known that they were going to take him anyway. Okay, maybe she would have. What she saw was heartbreaking, but also the happiest moment in her life. She just didn't want the sad part and was willing to give up the happy for the sad to not happen. She wrote the letter to tell Jared he had to move on without her, and they could never be more than friends.

'Fine, but you promise to show me what you saw all those years ago. And I promise this isn't a good memory to see. I've never talked about this with anyone and probably will never out loud. This is the best I can do, and I'm only doing it because it's you.' Jared looked at her, waiting for her to nod in agreement.

'I knew something was wrong the same day you gave me the letter. I found my father, and it was the first and only time I ever saw him cry, but until I looked back I didn't realize it. I was too focused on you. Something had happened, and you weren't the same.'

Jared stopped talking as memories of the day flashed before Cassie—like a movie. She had been crying, but she wouldn't tell him what was going on. When he got home, it was the only time he saw his father crying. Something had happened. The memory faded.

Jared was now standing in his house watching Ryder run around throwing things into a bag. They had to leave, and they had to leave immediately. Ryder went into action, but Jared couldn't move. He was standing in the doorway to his parent's room. His father had trashed the place, but that didn't stop Jared from staring where his mother should have been. He couldn't believe she was gone.

'Bro, we need to leave now,' Ryder interrupted Jared's thoughts. *'Dad gave me the address, and if we stay another minute, we're going to come face-to-face with Mikel.'*

Reaching down, Jared picked up his bag. He had already packed, and there was nothing more he needed. Jared looked one last time across the room to his mother's dresser. Her perfumes and jewelry were still sitting on it like she was going to return any time, even though the room was trashed. She wasn't going to return. Ever.

He left the house right behind his brother, running into the woods that were at the edge of their yard. Jared hefted his bag on his shoulder and kept pace with Ryder as he ran. He wanted to turn back and find Cassie one more time to tell her he was leaving, but they didn't have time, and he was pretty sure he didn't want to run into John either. Her uncle scared Jared as much as Nate's father.

Ryder led them into the woods farther and around town. Jared kind of knew where they were going, but he had no idea why his father told them to go there. It was just woods. How were they going to live in the woods? Ryder stopped as he made his way to the exact spot they were going to meet their father. Jared joined him and waited. Their father was late, but that was to be expected. He said he was meeting someone else first. Jared sat down in the shade of the trees as the sun set. Ryder chose to pace. He wasn't that good at waiting.

By the time darkness fell, Jared was ready to pass out. He had been up all day and now all night waiting for their father. They had to wait. There was nothing else they could do. When a flash of light caught their attention not too far down the hill, Jared was excited to finally see his father. Jared hurried ahead of Ryder this time. He needed to see that everything was fine. He needed his father to go back to being his father. Jared needed his dad now that his mother was gone.

Jared froze behind a large bush. His father was where the light was, but not as Jared expected. His father was tied down and not making any effort to escape. There was a man in a dark hooded cape walking around Jared's father. Jared didn't know what to do. His father wasn't trying to do anything to fight back. There wasn't time to think further before someone grabbed Jared and brought him into the light.

'Seems they found us,' the voice of the person holding Jared commented.

Jared thrashed in his arms. Something was off, really off.

'Jared. Stop,' his father commanded.

Jared immediately stopped and found Ryder not being held by anyone. Ryder stood and kept his eyes on the ground.

'We've been cast out by the clan. The wendigo have offered to take us in. This will be our family now,' his father said, still not trying to get out of the ropes.

From the shadows, more people appeared. There weren't as many as the skinwalker clan, but there were plenty of them to fight against. And it didn't look like Jared was going to get any help from his brother or father. Jared had heard enough about the wendigo to know they weren't safe. The wendigo were the bad guys.

'We can go alone,' Jared answered his father finally. He would rather be without a clan than be a wendigo.

'We might be able to make it, but your mother deserves vengeance.' His father's muscles bulged against the ropes as he spoke. 'The wendigo will help us get that. The skinwalkers sent her off to be killed because Mikel fears his son won't be the next alpha. He doesn't want it to be you. He sent your mother away to be killed. Don't let anyone tell you otherwise. The skinwalkers are dead to us. From today forward we will be wendigo.'

Jared stared at his father. It wasn't that simple. They were skinwalkers whether he wanted to be or not. At least, that is what Jared thought. He was completely wrong.

Images of that night played quickly: The moon rising and changing the older man into his animal totem, Jared's father being held down while partially transformed, the chanting and witches around his father preparing. Jared had to be restrained as they cut the skin right off the beautiful black leopard that was his father. His father grunted in pain but never screamed or cried out. Jared watched the scene in horror. By the time the night was done, his father was a wendigo.

It was more than Cassie could have imagined, and to know that her cousin had been planning to do that exact thing to Nate made Cassie want to run far away or puke. She wasn't sure which instinct called to her more. The whole wendigo world was more brutal than she wanted to be around.

'*There's more,*' Jared told her, bringing Cassie back to his memories. Taking a deep breath, she watched as the story continued.

Jared was twelve when his animal came. That was younger than most skinwalkers, and no one had expected it. It would be another two years before Ryder, his own twin, transformed for the first time. Jared was able to keep it a secret for three months before his father figured it out. For three months, the full moon came, and he was free of the life he was now living amongst the monsters. As a skinwalker and as a black leopard—like his father—Jared was able to sneak closer to town and find Cassie. Three times he was able to see her. Three times wasn't enough. He missed her more than anyone could tell or would ever know. Something about Cassie always drew Jared to her, but more once he was in his totem.

On the fourth full moon, Jared went down to the woods and expected to do the same, but that wasn't going to be the case. His father knew and had a plan of his own. Jared would never be able to join their new family—which his father was now the head of—until his animal was gone.

Ben Colley, Jared's father, looked completely different now. He was still the large blond man that Cassie remembered, but he was different. Anger and hate poured off him.

Jared tried to transform in his normal spot, looking forward to seeing Cassie again. He had been foolish and didn't notice the changes around him. As soon as he was in his animal form, he felt the magic bind him. He was frozen in his spot.

His father came from the woods with Michael, Cassie's uncle, beside him.

'*Jack needs to do this one,*' *Michael said in a voice which sounded identical to John's.*

Jack came from behind the two large men. There was nothing Jared could do. He had stepped right into the trap. He knew exactly how it was going to end, and his father would do nothing to stop it. Jared didn't even talk to them. There was no reasoning with his father. Jack's eyes danced excitedly as he stepped closer.

'Sorry, Son. This is going to hurt a bit, but you'll thank me in the end. To join the wendigo, you have to be one of us,' his father said as he leaned down and patted the cat head of Jared.

'With it being his first time, it will probably hurt more than normal,' Michael added.

Jared's father shrugged, like that didn't matter in the least to him.

'A little more won't change anything. Do it.' Ben walked away without looking back at Jared.

Jack grinned as his father handed him a knife.

Cassie pulled back, ending the connection between them without seeing anything more. Reaching up, Jared wiped the tear from her cheek.

"Your own father and my cousin did this to you?" she whispered in horror.

Jared's hand was still on her face as he stared at her, willing her to look inside his soul. Cassie closed her eyes and let more tears fall. She didn't see what they did to him, but after seeing what was done to his father, she already knew.

"You were beautiful," Cassie said quietly.

Jared chuckled. "I thought I was good enough. You never saw me."

"I didn't see you then." Cassie opened her eyes and gazed into his. She could still see the pain behind his eyes from reliving probably the worst day of his life.

Jared's brow furrowed in question.

"I saw your future when you were a skinwalker. That's

why I wrote the letter."

Jared came back to sit by Cassie and handed her the water she had asked for. Cassie knew he was anxious to hear her story and change the topic from his, but now they could both see that they were connected.

Grasping the bottle, Cassie took a long swig of it. She didn't want to go back to the memory she had buried for the past years, but Jared had shared his, and it was only fitting she did the same. The memory, for the most part, wasn't bad. It was the ending. She could still feel the pain from the first time she saw the end of the future for Jared. She didn't want to see it again. But she had made a promise.

When Jared held up the knife, Cassie took it and set it on the table. She didn't want him inside her head when she told him. She didn't want to cause him any more pain, or see the pain it had caused her. Being inside his head was intense and more than she thought it would be. She was used to catching glimpses and seeing things from people, but the feelings of being Jared were more than she ever felt off Whitney, who was the person she thought she knew the best. It was turning out that she might have known Nate and Jared even better than Whitney.

"I haven't thought of that day in eight years. When they took my memories away, they took away what I could do. They made me a loner without any friends and without any real memories."

Cassie shook her head. They took away a lot. All she could remember was that once John was nice to her and her life was different, but now she could remember more and knew that even that was a lie. Her life wasn't just better; it was a completely different life.

"Do you remember when Nate had to run back and be with his dad for part of the time during the festival?" Cassie asked. She sure remembered. Jared's face turned red. Yep, he remembered also.

"I think when you told me you were going to buy me a ring with a diamond as big as that bouncy ball, you must have triggered something in it, or I don't know."

"Man, I remember that. I was trying to be all suave and debonair. I thought if I told you that way, you would someday choose me instead of Nate. I didn't expect that you wouldn't understand." Jared ran his hands through his hair as he shook his head and laughed.

Jared had taken Cassie down an alley in town. He gave her a whole long speech about how he was going to grow up and be someone someday. He was going to be famous, and all he wanted was to have Cassie with him. She didn't have the slightest clue what he was talking about, but she could never imagine a world without her best friend in it, so she agreed with him. That's when he took out the ball he had won in one of the games. He got down on a knee, and in his own way proposed to Cassie, promising to buy her a ring as big as the ball someday. Cassie had no clue what he was talking about, and asked why he would need to buy her a ring. She didn't wear rings or jewelry. She hung out with two guys all the time. Jared covered up Cassie's confusion by dragging her off to the fortune-teller instead of explaining.

"I really had no clue why you were offering to buy me a ring," Cassie continued, and Jared laughed more.

Cassie paused as she thought more about the past and what she had seen. Seeing her hesitation, Jared reached over and took her hand. He gazed into her eyes and waited patiently for her to continue.

"I knew I was different before we went to the festival. I remember hearing everyone always talking about who they guessed my father was. Some people even guessed it was your dad or even Nate's dad since I hung around you guys all the time. I asked John once, and he reassured me that the person wasn't someone from town. John wasn't too forthcoming with anyone about the man since the man had broken the last alpha's law that my mother could never have a mate. He had never met the man before, and no one else had ever met him either.

"It doesn't matter now. In order to take the exam, I needed parental permission. I signed the papers without it, which means my parents are dead."

"Cas, I didn't know. I'm sorry." Jared rubbed the back of Cassie's hand.

She gave him a half smile and a shrug. "Doesn't matter much. It wasn't like they were coming back for me. They had sixteen years to change their minds."

"Cassie, don't talk like that. If your mother was anything like your aunt and uncle, she would have never stayed away by choice," Jared added.

Cassie shrugged again. She didn't know what to think now. While in her old life she felt like nothing had ever been told to her, she now had many memories of John and Maria searching for her mother and father over the years. They never found anything, but there were more than enough leads to keep them busy. Cassie was going to have to apologize to John later. How she told him that her mother was dead wasn't fair to him. He had never given up hope, and Cassie only knew a part of the extent he had gone to since she forgot eight years of her life.

"When we went to that fortune-teller, remember how she made us drink something? She said it would help her see the future." Jared nodded as Cassie remembered back to that day even clearer. "It didn't just help her see; it helped me. That was the first and only time I saw the future and not the past."

"You saw the future?" Jared asked.

"Not the future that happened. I saw what would have happened if you stayed with the skinwalkers. I saw what my life was supposed to be like. Not this stuff now. Something changed it all, and while I don't like that I lost my memories, and you had done what was done to you ..." Cassie couldn't even say out loud that his animal was skinned from him. "I'm glad it didn't turn out the way it was supposed to. I'm glad you're still alive."

Jared looked at her questioningly. "I'm missing something here. What did you see?"

Unable to reply, she closed her eyes as the image replayed in her mind just as it had that day.

Reaching up, he brushed her cheek. "Cassie, I want to know what you saw," he said quietly.

Cassie gazed into his brown eyes. He wasn't dead. He was right there with her. Cassie reached up, placing her hand on his chest. She could feel his heart beat beneath her hand. He was alive. He wasn't supposed to be alive. The future she saw was gone, and he was still there.

Grasping her hand, Jared kissed the back of it. "Please show me."

Cassie did know what to say. It had been eight years. She hadn't thought of that day in eight years, and now looking at him made it all much more real. This was the Jared she loved. This was the Jared she had lost.

"You've had enough pain in your life; you don't need to see something that never happened," Cassie replied, wanting to look away from him, but failing to do so.

"Cas, I want to see."

Searching his eyes again, she found that there were many questions behind his eyes. So much of his life he lost, and much changed. It did for Cassie also, but she didn't have to live with it for years. It was all new to her, but it wasn't for him. It was torment for eight years straight. He missed the skinwalkers and was constantly wondering what life would have been like. He wanted to see that Cassie was right, and the life he had was better for him. He needed to see it.

Hesitantly, Cassie picked up the knife. She didn't really want him to know all the emotion from that day, but he needed to realize that joining the wendigo wasn't all bad. There was one good thing that came from it. He was alive.

When she pricked her finger again and held it out for him, he sliced his hand without a second thought and took her hand in his. Cassie felt him as soon as they connected. It was easier the second time around. Closing her eyes, she tried to remember the day she wouldn't forget now that she had her memories back.

She had just grabbed Jared's arm and pulled him toward the booth that was near them. It had just opened. Cassie always loved fortune-tellers. She wanted to know how they did it and would study them as much as she could. She had grown better over the past two years at predicting things based on watching people, but the fortune-tellers were better than predicting. It was like they could actually see the future.

'Should we wait for Nate?' Jared asked as Cassie opened up the curtained doorway.

'No. He's been with his dad for forever. If we don't go now, someone else will, and we'll miss out,' Cassie complained.

She would have liked to have Nate there, but he was busy. He had grown busier and busier over the last year. His father was always taking him some place or another to meet important people. It wasn't what Nate wanted, but he couldn't tell his father no.

'Welcome,' the lady sitting behind the table said to them when they entered.

Cassie stepped forward to the table. This one was different than the last one her uncle took her to at the fair. The lady, dressed in all black, reached for a pitcher next to the table. After pulling out two cups, she poured a drink in them.

The curtain to the booth opened, and Cassie turned to complain that it was her turn. Nate stood in the doorway pouting.

'Hey. You guys said you wouldn't go to any booths without me,' he complained.

'You took too long.' Jared shrugged.

He was sticking up for him behind his back, but he never would to his face. Jared and Nate always had that sort of relationship. Cassie thought it was funny. They pretended to hate each other but were more like brothers than anything.

'I didn't take that long.'

'That long? We already made it around all the booths again, not playing at a single one because Cas insisted on waiting for you.'

Cassie turned back to the table and ignored them as they talked. The fortune-teller smiled at the two boys who were now bickering and pulled out a third cup.

'Well, obviously you did one. I found you guys in here,' Nate continued to complain.

'Cassie didn't want to miss her turn.'

'Ignore them. I usually do once they start arguing,' Cassie told her.

The lady laughed again. She poured a liquid which was dark in color into the glasses, then motioned for each to take one.

'I'm not supposed to take any drink without seeing them made. My uncle would kill me if I went against his orders,' Cassie informed the lady.

She smiled at Cassie. 'Wise words of wisdom from John's niece. I promise you there's nothing harmful in this. It's a homemade concoction I like to use that makes things easier to see with. If anything happens to you, tell him to find Sarah to blame instead of you. He has my phone number.'

Cassie stared at her. She was telling the truth. Why did her uncle have the phone number of the seer in the booth? That was odd. Cassie was going to ask, but Nate reached down and didn't hesitate to drink the liquid.

'It's actually kind of good,' Nate remarked.

Jared reached for one and did the same, not to be outdone by Nate.

Cassie glanced between them. Nothing was happening to either of them. It seemed safe enough, and if John knew the lady, then that had to be safe. Cassie was allowed to eat and drink other stuff at the festival. This booth was part of the festival and hence safe. At least, Cassie hoped so. Grabbing the drink, she tried to down it as quickly as the guys, but sputtered and gasped for air. The stuff was horrible. Jared and Nate began laughing. They had set her up on that one. Cassie turned and smacked each of them in the chest.

'Some best friends you guys are.'

The fortune-teller seemed to be enjoying the show as she waited.

'What is it you come here asking?' she finally asked Cassie.

'Me? Oh, I'm here for these two. They always are fighting. I think they want to know who's going to be stronger,' Cassie explained.

'I don't care,' Jared sputtered at the same time as Nate spoke.

'I don't need to know,' Nate added.

Cassie smiled at the fortune-teller. The lady turned back and took a box from behind her.

'My fortunes come from touching objects and transferring your essence to them. Each of you young men chose something from my box. Hold it in your hands for at least five seconds before putting it back.'

Nate gave Cassie one of his famous "you've got to be kidding me" looks before Jared beat him to it by picking something. Jared closed his hands around the small object and then returned it to the pile. Nate reached in and obviously chose the largest item in the box. His eight-year-old hands didn't even come close to closing around the metal object, but Cassie had no idea what it was. Nate tossed it back in the box.

'You too,' the lady prompted Cassie.

'But I didn't ask a question,' Cassie complained.

The fortune-teller smiled. 'Questions don't have to be spoken out loud. You heart knows your question.'

Cassie shrugged. She had tons of questions. Who was her father, for one? Where was her mother? Why hadn't they come back for her? What was it like to be an adult? When could she join the coven like Aunt Maria? Would Jess finally invite her to a sleepover? Did Cassie really even want to go to a sleepover with all girls? Sometimes they were nice at school, but other times they said stuff when they didn't think she could hear. Jared and Nate were all she needed, no matter what Uncle John and Aunt Maria tried to tell her. Cassie just wanted to spend the rest of her life with her two best friends. They were a team. All three of them. Together. Couldn't it stay that way forever?

Carefully, Cassie picked up a small silver-colored charm from the mixture of metal objects. She grabbed it thinking it was a flower, but it turned out to be a turtle. A cute little turtle. Cassie closed her hand around the charm and began to count to five. One. Two. Three. Four. Five.

Instantly she felt the world around her pause. Everything just stopped. Then as quickly as it stopped, it fast-forwarded. Cassie saw how the festival would end. John was going to step forward and ask some lady Cassie had never met to be his mate. Everyone was going to celebrate, but Cassie had no idea why. Months passed, and Cassie saw tidbits. Soon enough it was another fall celebration. This time, John was being named the next alpha. Mikel, Nate's father, was stepping down to raise Nate. John was taking over until Nate came of age. Again time fast forwarded to the next celebration. That year Cassie was the center of it all. They were naming Cassie the new seer for the clan. She had absolutely no idea what that meant, but everyone was happy about it. In a way, she was, too. She was finally joining the coven just like she wanted. But as she stood on that stage beside her uncle, she saw the faces of her two best friends. Nate and Jared were both appeared to be saddened by it. Cassie didn't understand. Why were they sad?

Time continued forward, and Cassie saw moment after

moment pass. Their disappointment came because the seer could never have a mate. A teenage Cassie was finally part of the coven, but set to be alone her whole life. When Nate announced he had chosen his mate, Cassie was sad. Their days as the three musketeers were going to end on his seventeenth birthday. She had to pretend to be happy for him. There weren't any other options.

Time continued to a specific spot where it stopped. Cassie was a teenager. Part of the coven, but very much alone. Nate had chosen his mate and moved on with his life as his father had ordered. But Jared wasn't that easy to sway. Cassie had tried to set him up with the friends she had made over the years, but Jared refused all of them. This one was too tall. This one was too sweet. This one had blond hair and the other not blond enough. He found a reason to reject every girl that had their eye on him.

Time slowed even further. It was like watching a movie now. Everything moved in real time.

'Jared, come back here,' Cassie called to her friend as he raced ahead on the path. They were out hiking the trails since Jared had offered to help Cassie collect the herbs she wanted for a new spell she was going to try.

Jared disappeared ahead of her. Cassie huffed, but she wasn't going to stop going. It was already getting close to dusk. She knew how to get to Shay's lookout, a hill that had the best views of the forest and hills along with the best spot to find Stonecrop in their area. Cassie kept going on the trail. It would be harder to get back in the dark, but that didn't matter. She needed the plant and didn't have time the rest of the week to go get it.

Cassie climbed ahead as the path took an upward slope. She was getting near the top, and there was just enough daylight to see by still. Cassie reached the spot and found the herbs to tuck into her bag. She turned to leave, but Jared jumped out of his hiding spot. Cassie didn't even startle.

'I knew you'd be there,' she told him. 'Seer. Remember?'

Cassie tapped her own head. She hadn't actually seen he would be hiding there, but she had spent most of her time with Jared—lately, even more than normal since Nate ditched them for his new mate.

'You did not,' Jared called her bluff.

Jared ran past Cassie, disappearing in a whirl. Standing still, she listened to the world around her. He was there. She could hear a movement every now and then, but he was sneaky, almost as sneaky as Nate. Cassie opened her eyes and sighed. Nate was no longer part of everything. He was moving on with his life, just like Jared was supposed to be doing.

'Hey, what's wrong?' Jared asked as he slowed down to look at her, grasping her hands in his own.

It was a simple gesture and one that he had done a million times, but Cassie felt now it meant more. Jared had become even more of a presence in her life, and she hated that she liked it. As seer, she could never have a mate. The coven and clan were her mates. Jared could never be. He was supposed to be moving on. If the clan found out, they would kick him out. Cassie had heard talk. Mikel was suspicious. Everyone was.

'You have to stop,' Cassie told him, pulling back her hand and turning away from him. He was on the pathway home. The only way she could go was up to the lookout spot.

Jared walked around her and took her hand back.

'I've told you before. I'm not going anywhere,' he told her, serious as ever.

'And as I've told you before, you need to pick a mate. Do you know how many girls in school watch your every move? They are waiting for their chance to be with you.' It hurt to say it, but Cassie needed him to understand. Everyone was waiting for him to choose someone. He was already eighteen, a year older than when Nate took his mate.

'I don't want a mate if I can't have you.'

Jared had been presenting that argument since the first

time Cassie told the guys what being seer meant. Nate was prepared for it, and his father wasn't going to let him disappoint anyone, but Jared didn't care. He wasn't giving up.

'Jared,' Cassie began, but his lips were already on hers. Cassie wasn't expecting him to do that and wasn't prepared to push him away. Her hands and mind betrayed her, and they held on tight to him.

It wasn't their first kiss and wasn't even the first that week. Jared was getting more and more bold. If the coven found out he had been trying to court Cassie, they would banish him, but he didn't care. Jared wasn't giving up.

Finally, Jared pulled back and sighed. 'It's almost night.'

Cassie looked into the sky. The moon was already out, but he was right. He was soon going to have to change.

'You have to give up on me,' Cassie begged him. 'I don't want you to be thrown out of the clan. I'd rather see you every day with someone else than see you turn into one of them.'

Everyone who had left the clan only had one place to go: the wendigo. Cassie didn't know about them when she was little, but over the past four years, she had learned a lot. Her clan had a rival one—the wendigo—and they hunted down and initiated every cast out skinwalker to their cause. Cassie was still unsure if they were willing or not, but no matter what, the wendigo were bad people and Cassie didn't want Jared anywhere near them.

'I will never give up on you.'

Leaning down, he softly brushed his lips to Cassie's. Just that simple gesture made her stomach flutter. No matter how she tried to stop liking Jared, it would never happen. He was the last thing in her world that was still real, still hers and only hers.

'Shoot. Time's up.' Jared stepped back two steps. Black fur erupted around him as he changed into four legs instead of two. His clothing lay shredded at his feet.

'*You know how your mother hates when you do that,*' Cassie scolded him.

Cat Jared jumped at her and knocked her to the ground, expertly pinning her beneath him without harming a single hair on her body. Cassie huffed at him while humor twinkled behind his eyes.

'*Let me up,*' she complained.

Cat Jared leaned down and licked her with his large, wet, cat tongue.

'*Ew, come on,*' she whined more.

Cat Jared smiled at her. While a normal person would be afraid of a pure black leopard holding them to the ground, Cassie was still giving him a stare down. Cat Jared opened his mouth to lick Cassie again.

'*Okay, okay, fine. I get it. Don't scold the huge, scary cat.*' *Cassie knew exactly what Jared wanted her to say.*

The large cat moved back and let Cassie stand. She turned and contemplated sticking her tongue out at him, but he would tumble her to the ground again. She was never going to win against Jared in his cat form. Cassie turned back to grab her bag and head back. Jared stood on the path, blocking her. Cassie moved to pass him, but he just countered.

'*What now?*' she asked him. '*You know this always goes a bit better when you talk to me before you become a cat.*'

Jared lowered his cat head and butted Cassie's leg. She wasn't going to get past him unless he wanted to let her. Cassie turned around, and cat Jared walked beside her, urging her to go to the cliff. Cassie walked along with him, making it to the overlook in time to see the lights turn on in the houses in the country. Jared sat down, and Cassie did the same. There weren't many houses, but it was fun to see the little sparks of light here and there. Jared moved behind Cassie, and she leaned back to use him as a pillow. He hummed beneath her like always. She looked up at the sky. She wasn't cold with Jared keeping her warm.

Silence was hard with anyone but him. With Jared, it was easy. She was used to sitting around with him in his cat form as he had been stopping by since he first changed. She didn't feel the need to talk. Instead, she watched the sky, hoping for a shooting star to wish upon. Her wish would always be the same. She would wish for a different life, and one where she could have a mate and a future. She didn't want to be the seer. She didn't want to see the future. All she wanted was a future. A real one. Beside Jared.

CHAPTER 7

Cassie broke her connection with Jared and caught her breath. Everything had seemed very real. It felt real. She even found herself trying not to stare at Jared's lips. The kiss was even more real than the one she had with Nate even a moment before. It was just a version of the future that never happened, but she knew what it felt like. She glanced up and caught him staring at her.

"Hey, that wasn't too bad," Jared told her.

Cassie shook her head no. She didn't finish the memory with him in it. She couldn't. Cassie closed her eyes. She didn't want him to see the tears she knew would come. He had shown her what she wanted to know. She had to finish her memory for him.

"That wasn't all I saw then," Cassie added quietly.

"Did we end up mated?" Jared guessed, more like hoped.

Cassie shook her head no.

"The day after that, you left home looking for a way to be my mate. You never returned. Your father found you later. You had been killed for not staying within the skinwalker borders. I never saw you alive again. You died because I never told you to go away. You died because I held on and didn't let you go like Nate. You died because of me."

The tears came as she felt the memory and saw him in a casket. It never came to be, but she knew deep down that was Jared's fate. He was always going to die if he didn't give her up. It was her fault. She led him on. She always kissed him back. If she hadn't done that, if she had stayed away as she had from Nate like his father had asked, Jared

120

would have moved on. Jared would have found a mate, and he would have been happy. Jared would have lived.

"That's why I went right home after the festival and wrote you that letter. I was saying good-bye because I knew you wouldn't let me go otherwise. I had to be strong enough. I had to let you go so you wouldn't die. I never had a vision like that before, but I knew your fate was death if you stayed with me."

"But that was just one version of the future. Obviously, there were other possibilities," Jared tried to reason.

"Possibilities? Yes, always. But I knew that if I didn't let go of you, then you would die." Cassie opened her wet eyes to look at him.

The vision had felt real, and she remembered every detail. She could see his dead body. She remembered touching his dead face. It was too much to bear. Even just thinking of it hurt. She had loved him.

She finally understood the mating bond. She had truly loved both him and Nate at one time. She knew why she was able to bond to them now. Her mind might not have remembered, but fate did. Jared and Nate were once the most important people in her life.

"But I'm here now," Jared added, wiping away a tear.

She nodded. "Yeah, but not all of you."

Cassie thought of the great big black leopard he was. He was beautiful and fit in the nighttime perfectly. While people thought black panthers were all black, Cassie knew that he still had spots, just dark spots on a dark background. His fur was soft, and even as a giant cat he could walk through the night unseen and unheard. He was a majestic animal. But it didn't matter. He had been skinned, and his totem was gone.

"I don't remember that much. It's been years, and I only transformed a few times before my father took it from me." Jared spoke like he didn't care, but Cassie knew better. He cared more than he would ever let on. She had been in his memory, and she would never forget that.

Rising, Jared walked to the door.

"Twindar," he teased as Cassie gave him a look.

He always called it 'twindar' when he could tell where Ryder was, but Cassie had a feeling it was more than being twins. Nate seemed to know where people were all the time, too. It was more like 'night human-dar', but that was a mouthful. Jared opened his bedroom door.

"Um," Ryder said as he looked at Cassie. "Dad ..." Ryder stopped like he was unsure if he should say anything else.

Jared shrugged. "She's going to be my mate, bro, get over it," he teased his tongue-tied brother.

Ryder shook his head and directed his gaze at Jared. "Dad insists you bring Cassie to supper to verify that she's marked as your mate," he quickly said.

"Shit," Jared muttered as he locked his fingers together on his head, like he was stretching and relaxing, but that was far from the case.

"Yeah, I know. I told him I saw it and all, but you know how he is," Ryder explained.

Jared shrugged. "Guess I expected he would want to see it, but I was kind of hoping he would just look at it through your eyes."

"Umm." Ryder stared back at Cassie again.

Smiling, Cassie shook her head. It seemed like the wendigo might have the same problem as the skinwalkers when it came to her.

"He tried, didn't he?" Cassie guessed.

Ryder's eyes got big because she'd guessed correctly.

"Whitney said that Mikel couldn't see me either. None of the skinwalkers can see me in the eyes of the others," Cassie explained. "I don't know why, maybe a night human thing. Don't ask me. I'm new to all of this."

Jared reluctantly nodded. After he had nodded back, Ryder turned to go across the hallway to his room, and Jared shut the door behind him.

"I guess I get to meet your dad … rather, see him again after many years," Cassie added. She had seen enough of him in Jared's memory to not really want to meet him again, but it wasn't like they could say no. He was now the alpha of the wendigo. She had to assume he had the same power as Nate's dad.

"I'd rather not, but you get it." Jared didn't look too enthusiastic about it.

"When do we have to go?" Cassie asked. She was comfortable where she was but had the feeling you didn't keep an alpha waiting.

Jared glanced back at his clock on his desk. "I'd say we have maybe five or ten minutes."

Cassie nodded and stood. "I'll go get Nate."

Jared's eyes grew wide. "I don't think my father wants to see him now, or maybe even ever."

'And I don't think I'll ever leave you alone with two wendigo alphas,' Nate said in her mind.

He was awake and walking into her thoughts as easily as she just remembered her memories.

'How long have you been up?' Cassie wondered how much Nate had heard of what she and Jared had shared.

'Since the other wendigo came back,' Nate replied.

Cassie heard him walking noisily down the stairs, so she sat back down.

"I don't think you get in choice in him coming." Cassie shrugged when Nate came into the room. The tiger was almost as large as the futon Cassie was sitting on. Heck, maybe even a bit bigger.

Jared stared at Nate. Nate glared back at him with his tiger eyes, willing Jared to challenge him.

Jared gave a shrug. "Your funeral."

'Ask him if he trusts his dad to not do something to you, one-hundred-percent trusts him.'

Cassie looked at Jared. "Do you trust your father completely to not do something to me?"

Jared paused. He was debating with himself. "I guess."

'See. That's why I'm coming with. If he trusted him, he would have answered right away.'

Nate was right, but Cassie didn't need to tell him that. From what she had seen, she didn't trust Jared's father. Nate coming with them might upset him, but she would feel safer. Jared was a wendigo beneath his father. He would have to follow any command, and Cassie wasn't sure that Ben was exactly stable. He could outright order Jared to kill her, and she'd have no way to defend herself. Yes, Nate had to come with them.

"You guys agreed to a truce, right?" Cassie asked, looking first at Jared and then tiger Nate. Both nodded to Cassie. "Then get along well enough to keep that truce. If it's safer for Nate to stay here, then he will. But if not, he comes."

'I will not,' Nate protested mentally, but Cassie ignored him. She needed Jared to make choices and not force his hand. She needed Jared and Nate to be friends again. Their life worked much better that way.

Jared thought for a moment, and Cassie didn't need to read his mind to know that she made sense.

"Fine. I don't trust my dad," Jared remarked.

That was an understatement. He was the one who turned Jared into a monster instead of the beautiful black jaguar he really was supposed to be. He's the one who caught him and let Jack skin him. He was the one looking for vengeance above all else. If his dad, for any moment, had cared about him, he would have never taken Jared's totem or his future away from him.

Jared walked to the doorway and opened his room door.

"Then follow me," he said as he led the way out.

Cassie paused. She didn't really want to leave the safe barrier of the room. Stopping, Jared turned back to Cassie and offered her his hand.

"I won't let him hurt you," Jared promised her.

'Neither will I. No matter if you have his mark on you or not. I found you first. You are my mate, and I'll protect you forever,' Nate added. *'Take his hand and pretend to play your part. I don't know what Ben is planning, but we need to tread carefully with him. He's very smart and cunning. Always has been. We've had several run-ins with him over the past few years. We need to play this cautiously.'*

Cassie turned back to Nate and touched his head. She smiled as she looked at him now with all her memories intact. Jared had always defended her as best he could, but he was a bit smaller than Nate. When it came to a fight, Nate was the one who made sure Cassie never got hurt. They didn't have all the past she remembered, and Nate still didn't seem to remember it, but Cassie did. Nate's personality was one that protected people. It was a risk to leave the room, but she trusted him. He would keep her safe, and in the life she should have had, he always kept his word on that.

Reaching through the spell, she took Jared's hand. She didn't need to read his mind to see his jealousy, but that was nothing new. That had been their lives since they were little. Nate was jealous of Jared, and Jared jealous of Nate. Each one wanted what the other had, and nothing was going to change that … well, at least, Cassie thought nothing would. Now she saw the weird truth. They both had what each other wanted. Jared was now next in line to be alpha, and so was Nate. They always said they both couldn't be alpha. The joke was on them.

Swiftly, Jared led the way back through the house and turned down a hallway Ryder hadn't shown Cassie. She wondered where they were going, but she kept quiet as Nate padded along beside her. It didn't take long to make it to the doorway of where they must have been going, because Jared stopped at the closed door. He looked at Cassie and then to Nate. The guys locked eyes and nodded.

Jared pushed open the doorway with his free hand and took Cassie into a large dining room. It was out of place. The whole house was normal and cozy, maybe a few thousand square feet at the most. The dining room, though, was easily the size of the rest of the house. It was more of a banquet show-off room than anything. Right now the room had one long table in it that could have seated over twenty people. High backed, ornately carved chairs lined both sides with an even larger chair poised at the end. It was occupied by a man who was so large that it looked like he had to squeeze into a chair that both Cassie and Whitney could have sat in at the same time.

Ben Colley glanced up from his food as they entered. His light blue eyes watched them and turned to a glare as Nate came in the room. He did his best to hide it, but Cassie saw it.

"Glad to see your brother gave you the message," Ben said as they came closer.

Jared nodded as Cassie saw that the table had two more settings at it, across from each other and on each side of his father. Jared walked over to the nearest chair and pulled out the one next to it and further from his father. He nodded to Cassie, and she sat in it. Jared then pulled out his own chair and pushed his plate and cup down for Cassie, keeping her away from his father. Jared reached across the table and took the second set of dishes for his own place.

Ben watched his son and then began laughing. Normally, Cassie liked to hear people laugh, but not the blond man at the end of the table. Something about his laugh gave her goose bumps. Maybe it wasn't even his laugh. It was him in general. He might have been smiling and laughing, but there was no happiness in him. His eyes told everything, and Cassie didn't need more than the glance she got. She kept her focus on the plate of food before her. Ben Colley was evil and not just a little bit. Everyone had some evil in them. No one was just good or bad. But he was as close to all bad as one could get.

"Ahh, dear Son, why don't you let me and your mate get

to know each other a little better?" Ben said, casually motioning to the seat next to him.

"You have a little problem with witches, Father, and I feel better with her on this side of me," Jared replied, not even playing into the pretending.

Ben smiled. "I can't help it if witch blood tastes good."

Jared looked up at his father, and his father smiled back at him. There was no love between the two of them.

"You'll find out soon enough, Son. For your sake, hopefully, you won't suck her dry." Ben reached down and took a large piece of steak and shoved it in his mouth.

Nate growled at Ben, and he laughed again.

"Cute pet. I hope it's house broken." Ben grinned with a mouthful of food.

Cassie looked at the food before her, and her appetite was gone. It had actually faded the moment she walked into the room, but his talk of bleeding her dry was enough to make any lingering bit of hunger disappear.

Jared turned to her and mouthed the words 'I'm sorry'. Her hands were still at her side, and he reached for the closest one.

"Do show," Ben commanded. "I had a hard time believing Ryder when his mind was completely blank of any images of your mate. I had to think it was another imaginary friend he was talking about."

Jared ground his teeth as he lifted up Cassie's marked hand to show his father. As soon as his father could see it, Jared dropped their hands back beneath the table.

"Miss Cassandra, you will have to forgive my son and his rudeness. He hates to be ordered around, but until he can show he's stronger than me, I have to remind him from time to time." Ben kept eating, but now Jared wasn't picking up his own fork.

Ben paused shoveling the food into his mouth for long enough to finally notice that both Cassie and Jared were just sitting there.

"Eat this well-cooked food," he ordered again.

Jared's hand shook as he picked up his fork. Cassie didn't move. She had no appetite. Ben raised an eye at her as she sat there staring at her plate.

'Cassie, eat something before he realizes you don't have to follow his orders,' Nate told her through their bond.

'What?' Cassie asked. She wasn't a wendigo. Alpha status didn't matter to her.

'As Jared's mate, you have to follow his alpha just like him. If you don't, it proves you are stronger than him. As soon as he figures that out, there's going to be a fight to get out of here,' Nate explained just as quickly as before.

Cassie was still learning the basics of everything, but she trusted Nate. And what he said made sense. There was no argument in her. Getting out alive sounded like the best plan. She'd keep her questions for later.

She shakily reached for her fork, dropping Jared's hand in the process. Jared didn't look over at her as he chewed the piece of food in his mouth very slowly. Each bite seemed to brew more anger in him toward his father. They were now locked in a staring match. Cassie raised a piece of the food to her mouth, but she still didn't want to eat it. It got closer, and she could feel the sprinkling of magic on it.

'It's laced with magic,' Cassie said to Nate. He jumped up, and with a swipe of his paw hit the food to the ground, splattering it everywhere and knocking Jared's food over in the process.

Jared stopped his chewing and stared at the mess.

Ben smiled at the mess. "Part bloodhound I see."

Cassie looked back at Nate. He was still sitting behind her with his lips raised and a low growl in his throat. Jared spit his food out.

"First rule of witchcraft," Cassie said quietly as Jared looked at her, "never eat anything that has magic on it."

With the food all on the floor, Ben's order faded. Jared turned back to his father.

"What are you trying to do to us now?"

Ben shrugged. "I figured a love potion couldn't hurt anything."

Jared continued to glare at his father. "She has my mark," Jared replied.

"And his didn't go away," Ben observed.

Cassie reached up and rubbed her neck. She hadn't pulled her hair up and had no clue how Ben knew that.

"I figure it's a race to bond to her, and since you insist on falling in love, a little magic would be needed," Ben explained, like it was obvious.

"I don't need magic, Father. She has all her memories back," Jared told him.

Ben smiled, and this was the first time Cassie thought it might actually be genuine.

"That makes things a bit easier for you. We'll do the ceremony tonight to bond you to her."

"That's too soon," Jared complained.

His father silenced him with one look. "Tonight you'll join my ranks as my second-in-command, one way or another. Bond to her if that's what you want, or we kill her and her tiger. Choice is yours."

Ben nodded to Jared as if dismissing him. Rising, Jared took Cassie's hand to lead her away.

Cassie glanced back as they neared the doorway. Ben was sitting there, still smiling at them.

"And, Son, you'd do best to remember this is an order. You bind, or you kill her. It will be a celebration tonight. We can celebrate your first tasting of witch blood. I promise you, Son, you'll never steal blood from the hospital again." Ben raised a glass full of dark red liquid to them as Jared pulled Cassie away.

Cassie was more than happy to pass the barrier back into Jared's room. Dinner wasn't exactly inviting, and she felt more and more unsafe with the alpha wendigo as they sat there. Ben was creepy, and by how he was talking she got the feeling that he would prefer Jared kill her instead of bonding with her. Cassie sure didn't feel safe anywhere.

"Sorry about my dad," Jared apologized as he dropped her hand and went over to a mini-fridge beneath his desk. He pulled out several sandwiches.

"Stocked up?" Cassie asked, sitting down on the futon and hoping her nerves would settle. Nate sat down right next to her feet and laid his head on the seat next to her, keeping Jared from sitting down beside her.

"Most of the meals with me and my father end that way. Thanks for keeping us from eating that." Jared nodded to Nate, then placed all the food on the table in front of Cassie.

Cassie reached for a sandwich and opened it, but Nate leaned forward and licked it quickly before it could go to her mouth.

"Ew," she complained and handed him the food. Tiger Nate swallowed it down in one bite. "If you wanted one, you could just tell me."

Tiger Nate grinned at her and flipped his tail on the rest of the sandwiches.

Jared unwrapped one and sat at his desk in the chair backward to face them. She handed another sandwich to Nate before grabbing one for herself.

Cassie ate in silence as she thought. They were being backed into a corner with the whole bind or be killed stuff from Ben. She knew it was impossible for her to bind to someone if she were already bonded, but no one knew that was the case. They all thought Nate was just picked as her mate and wasn't really her mate yet.

'We have to tell him,' Cassie told Nate as he woofed down yet another sandwich.

'I was thinking the same thing,' Nate replied.

'Did you finally get your memories back?' Cassie asked.

'No, but if you trust him, then I have to.'

"So the whole binding thing …" Cassie began.

Jared stared at her, waiting for her to say more. She looked at Nate and then at the food.

"Nate and I are already bonded," Cassie spat out as fast as she could.

Cassie didn't want to look up and see Jared's face. He would be mad and maybe even a little sad. She waited for a second to see if the mating bond with him would tell her how he felt. Nothing came across. She couldn't help it. She glanced up, and she immediately felt bad. She had all the memories of their past now and what their future might have been. She knew exactly what Jared was feeling. He was crushed. She had to explain.

"When Jack made me make the potion, I didn't tell you guys that the secret ingredient to it was my blood. One of the wendigo had attacked me the day before, and Nate had used his blood to heal me. When I was forced to prove the potion, I had to add my blood to it and ended up bonded to Nate. It wasn't intentional, and no one knows. My aunt put a covering spell on it to keep it hidden. Now I don't know what we can do about tonight because you can't defy what your dad orders you to do." Cassie spoke quickly, but it wasn't like she had to be slow. Both the guys had super hearing.

"No one can defy my dad," Jared replied quietly, not even commenting about the bonding.

"I can, but that doesn't do us any good," Cassie added.

"Cas, why did you bind to him?" Jared asked, and Nate growled. Jared was more sad than angry with Cassie, but as he looked at Nate, the anger flashed behind his eyes again.

"I didn't want to, and he wasn't going to make me do it. He already told the coven no when they tried to do it after I got hurt." Cassie thought back to just days before Nate told the leader of the coven that he wouldn't do it. And Cassie remembered the words she heard back. "Shoot."

"What?" Jared asked at the same time as Nate.

'What?'

Cassie laughed. It wasn't that it was funny, and she wasn't happy. She just didn't know how else to respond. Her life just kept getting worse by the moment.

"When Nate didn't bind to me in front of the coven, he made them a promise. If I ended up bonding to the wendigo, then it's his job to hunt me down and kill me. Now your father says if I don't bond to you, you will have to kill me. Either way, one of you has to kill me. Life sucks. This whole night human world crap is the worst, but this is just icing on the cake." Cassie shook her head as she got out one last laugh.

"If I free you guys, you won't last long. They're still tracking Maria each day and are getting closer to getting her. There's no clan or witches to protect you. Running means certain death. Why in the world would fate allow you to choose a person as a mate if you were already bonded to another person?" Jared was now standing and pacing around the room. His anger was gone, and he was genuinely concerned about the situation.

'If there was only a way to trick Ben and gain more time. Once John frees the witches, we will be safe. Your uncle has talked to me several times, and they are safe. He can't explain much, but they have to keep changing locations,' Nate explained. *'We can't join them right now. But it won't be long before he gets to the witches. Then the coven will be back, and we will be safe. We just need more time.'*

Cassie looked between her two friends. It was ridiculous that one would have to kill her, but she had each of their marks on her. Here she wanted no mates. Now had two and one would have to kill her no matter what she did. Fate stunk.

Leaning back over the futon arm in frustration, she let out a loud sigh and stared at the doorway behind her.

"Ahh," she complained. "This isn't fair. First, I'm an outcast with no memory of my past. Now I remember, and it doesn't matter. It doesn't change anything. I wish I knew more. Aunt Maria knew exactly what to do, and I can't talk to her because if I do, the wendigo will kill her, but without her, I will die. Life isn't fair."

She was being dramatic, but Cassie was stuck. Her life wasn't anything like she wanted, and time and time again she felt like she had no control. Everyone around her was making choices for her. Cassie stared at the doorway, but the bag sitting next to it caught her eye. The witch supplies were in that bag.

"Well, I could temporarily break the bond," Cassie suggested. It would buy time like Nate wanted, but she wasn't completely sure she could.

"You can what?" Jared asked in shock.

'When you said you were working on getting out of it, was this what you meant?' Nate asked at the same time.

Both guys were in shock, but Nate was also hurt. Cassie felt a bit sorry for him. It wasn't like she didn't like him, and to remember her past correctly, she now harbored very little hate for him. He had been her best friend, but he had been lied to and had his memories erased just like hers. Nate was just as much of a victim as she was.

"This summer I met someone who wanted to break a blood bond. I was able to make a spell that worked for them for a short time. I can try to do the same. For as much as I know, it can't be permanently undone, and I don't know how long it will last but it's something, right?" Cassie clarified.

'Explain more,' Nate responded. He needed details as his mind went instantly to planning.

Jared was now pacing the room, rubbing his forehead in thought. Cassie trusted Jared. He would never let her get hurt, but he was a wendigo now. He had to obey his father, and Cassie wasn't certain she should share everything with him.

'I broke the blood bond between two people because the guy was afraid that if he died, then his bonded would die

also, and her family was trying to kill him. When he got injured, he was able to bond to a second person. It all happened really fast. I don't know how long undoing the bond would work. They chose to bond back together, so I can't be certain it would last hours, days, months, or years. From everything I read, you can't break the bond forever, but a temporary break is possible. I think something like how you were blocking the bond to keep me from getting the wounds they were doing to you.'

'Could you make enough to break the bond with Jared once I have everyone safe?' Nate asked.

That was exactly what had happened over the summer. Once Devin was healing, he rebonded to his girlfriend, Nessa. Cassie liked the idea of not being bonded to anyone, but had a feeling the spell didn't work that way. She would have to choose someone, and since the wendigo, besides Jared, scared the crap out of her, she was pretty certain it would have to be Nate.

'We could make this work for us. You break our bond, and I go help your uncle free everyone. Once they're is safe, I can come back for you, and you can break your bond to him and rebond to me.' Tiger Nate was nodding his head.

"What is he saying?" Jared asked as he stopped his pacing and watched them.

'Tell him I agree with him, and I won't be breaking my oath to the coven.'

"He thinks I should do it. His promise to the priestess didn't cover if I join you guys right now. As long as I'll be back to him some day, then technically I'm not joining you guys completely," Cassie replied, leaving out their whole previous conversation.

Jared nodded.

"That could work. My father insisted that you bind to me tonight or die. He never said you had to bind to me forever." Jared wanted forever, but he was more concerned with Cassie dying at the hands of his bloodthirsty father.

"Is it settled?" Cassie asked, looking between the tiger on one side of her and the young man on the other.

"Yes."

'Yes.'

CHAPTER 8

"I think that should work," Cassie said to the empty room.

Jared was with his father making preparations for the ceremony, and Nate was upstairs asleep. He wanted to rest up before he went to help John and Maria. He wouldn't explain, but he claimed they knew more and were almost ready for his assistance.

Cassie took an eye dropper from the kit and opened up her necklace. She had been wearing the empty vial since her trip with Whitney, and it made much more sense now. The old seer had insisted Cassie take the vial necklace when they left her, but she had no clue why. The seer told her to wear it until she needed it. Cassie put a few drops of the potion into the vial and closed it back up. There would be enough to cut the bond between her and Jared if needed, but she didn't know if that was possible. You could only bond with one person, and the only time she saw it work before, the person who had been unbonded with died, so they never had to see what would happen if you bonded twice. Cassie had more questions and no one to talk to. Again, she wished for Maria to just show up and help her.

Unfortunately, she didn't have time to analyze everything. Time was running low, and Ben was serious when he said he would order Jared to kill Cassie if they didn't bond.

After gently setting the vial on the table, Cassie went to find Nate. She still didn't know how he planned to sneak off and help her aunt and uncle.

Tiger Nate was sprawled out, taking up the whole bed,

and she laughed to herself. He was a tiger in shape, but still so Nate in attitude. If she had her memories the whole time, she would have been able to guess the tiger she met was Nate, not Whitney. She knew him really well now. She knew Jared well, too.

Cassie had to hope John and Maria could get everyone out, and Nate would come back. She had yet to see a female in the wendigo camp, and her gut told her that wasn't a good thing.

Tiger Nate opened one eye and looked at Cassie as she stood there thinking and watching him at the same time.

"I think I got it done," she told him.

The tiger nodded to her and closed his eye again. Cassie tried not to laugh out loud. Her life had grown a bit surreal. Nate lifted up his large tiger head and stared at her as if to question her laugh.

"Please don't give me that look. Had you told me two weeks ago I would be sitting around talking to a real live tiger, I would have called the psych ward at the hospital for you. This is all too crazy."

Tiger Nate rolled off the bed without as much as a thunk of the floor and padded his way over to the bathroom, but paused in the doorway.

Cassie giggled more. "Please don't tell me that you need to use the restroom and need me to lift the toilet seat."

Tiger Nate rolled his eyes.

'Come with me please.' He finally spoke.

Cassie followed him into the bathroom. Luckily it was as large and ornate as the bedroom, and they easily both fit in it. Cassie had to scold herself from thinking about how if she invited tiger Nate into her bathroom at home there wouldn't be enough room. It would be hilarious, though.

'Close your eyes if you don't want to catch an eyeful,' Nate warned her.

'An eyeful of what?' Cassie asked as the tiger stood back onto two feet and began to morph into a human.

Cassie shut her eyes and put her hands over them. Skinwalkers transformed back naked, and Nate was standing there, facing her. Her cheeks flushed since he was naked in the bathroom with her.

"I'm decent now," Nate stated, removing her hands from her closed eyes.

She peeked through her lashes. He was standing in front of her with just a towel wrapped around his waist. His chest was bare, but no longer cut up. There wasn't even a scar left from his fight two days with the wendigo. Cassie tried not to get caught staring at him. He looked good.

He continued to hold her hands as he stood there waiting for her to fully open her eyes.

"You shouldn't be human. You know Jack is trying to catch you," Cassie scolded, finally bringing herself out of her gawking and back to reality.

"And that's why we're in the bathroom. He came into the bedroom, but not the bathroom. He couldn't have placed a holding spell here," Nate told Cassie logically.

Reaching up, she touched his face where the last cut had been when he was human. His whole body had been slashed, but she hated to see the cut not healing on his cheek. It was gone now, but she could still see exactly where it had been. His cheek was rough from not shaving in several days. Nate closed his eyes at her touch and made a low noise in his throat, almost like a purr.

Nate took Cassie's hands up to his lips and kissed her fingertips.

"I have to leave soon. I wouldn't do it if it wasn't necessary. I hate to leave you alone with the monsters. I know Jared will do everything to keep you safe, but I still hate it."

"I'll be fine," Cassie told him. She had to hope she would be. Otherwise, he would feel her doubt through the bond just as much as she could feel his regret at leaving.

"Why did you chance turning human?" Cassie changed

the subject. His blue eyes sparkled as they stared at her. All she could feel was love, though she couldn't tell whether it was her own or his through the bond.

"When you cut the bond, I won't be able to talk to you in your head anymore, and I won't be able to turn back human until the witches are back. I won't be able to do this."

Nate pulled Cassie closer and gently pressed his lips to her. She would have been surprised had she not been thinking the exact same thing. His lips were soft as they brushed against hers. Reaching up, she put her hands gently on his face to keep him from pulling back. Nate took that as a sign to continue and wrapped his arms around her, tugging her closer to him. Her one hand drifted down, and she placed it on his bare chest. Nate slowly pulled back and rested his forehead against hers.

"It kills me to have to leave you. It's worse to know you're going to bond to another guy. Cas, I don't have your memories of the past, but I do have a million memories of watching you over the years. My father said I had to stay away from you, but that never meant I couldn't watch. We were friends once, and I loved you back then. I still love you and will even after you bind to Jared. I know this is all messed up, but once everything gets sorted out, I promise you, you will have as much time as you need to figure out what you want. I want you. That will never change. But I respect you and know this is more than could be asked of anyone. Please don't give up on the night human world. Please don't give up on us. Please don't give up on me." His last words were barely above a whisper. His blue eyes stared intensely at her, willing her to love him back. And she did, even if she couldn't say it.

Cassie could feel the sadness of her running away from him days ago as he was afraid she would leave again. They were in the middle of a war with another clan, but Nate was still worried about her running away. He was serious about every word he'd spoken. The Nate from her vision gave up on her and left. This wasn't the same Nate, and she had to remember that. Fate was changed, and her life was still up in the air.

Nate pulled back and nodded.

'Jared's coming upstairs,' Nate told her mentally as he stepped back and instantly melted into his tiger form, the towel dropping to the ground.

He left the bathroom as silently as he came. She stood there with the sinking feeling that Nate's kiss was one of good-bye. The bond, as annoying as it was, would be gone. There would be nothing left tying her to the life she had growing up. All the witches were gone, all the skinwalkers were gone, her aunt and uncle were gone, and her best friend was gone. Everything was all messed up. It made Cassie want to lock herself in the bathroom and cry. She didn't want everything to change. She would have never taken the test if she'd known this was what it was going to turn out like. Cassie took a deep breath.

'I will never leave you, Cassie, whether the bond is there or not,' Nate told her, feeling exactly what she was feeling. *'And this isn't good-bye. I just needed to get a reminder kiss in for you. I don't remember Jared, but from your eyes, I can see that you think he's a good person. I needed to be sure you don't forget me when you bind to him. I'll always be here. I love you.'*

Cassie sucked in a deep breath. She didn't need to hear the words, as she felt it across the bond from the moment she returned to town, but it made her stomach flip-flop. She didn't want to fall for anyone; she wanted to be free. Nate wasn't trying to force her to stay around. He was going to let her go find her way in the world. Every time she thought she had it figured out, someone had to throw her off balance.

"Are you okay?" Jared asked from the doorway.

Cassie looked into the mirror and saw that there were tears on her cheeks. She quickly wiped them away.

"I'm fine," she added, reaching down and patting some

cool water on her face. "Just worried."

Coming back into the room, she saw Nate lounging on the bed just as she had found him before.

"Did you not get the potion to work?" Jared asked, worry seeping into his voice.

"No, that's fine. Did you find out more about Jack's plans?" Cassie asked, changing the subject. She was getting good at that with these two guys.

"Yeah. I was able to get down there early enough to overhear his meeting with my father. He's convinced that you can be bonded to the clan. He claims the reason they don't let the seer have a mate is because she's the only person who can have more than one. If she has more than one mate, it throws the balance off to everyone. With such a valuable position, people are afraid to punish any seer who does that, and hence, they found it easier to just rule out any mate for the seer of the coven," Jared explained.

'Makes sense,' Nate added.

"Then what do we do?" Cassie replied. It did make sense to her. She had two mates, and she was next in line to be seer. Jared seemed to know a whole lot for not being part of the coven.

"Nothing. Jack's plans can't work since all bonds are made on the fact that the binding has to be mutual. You can't bind to someone you don't want to be bonded to. He keeps forgetting that part."

"I'm pretty sure I didn't want a mate, or two of them, and yet here I am," she pointed out. It wasn't that she didn't find both of the guys attractive; she just didn't want to be married at sixteen.

"Touché," Jared replied with a wink.

'I think you may be right. You may need to bind earlier and go to the meeting ready to face off with Jack. I have a feeling he won't bow down easily to not getting his way,' Nate replied.

"Nate thinks we should bind earlier and then go to the

ceremony," Cassie told Jared.

Jared rubbed his chin as he thought.

"That should work. If we do the bond now, it's still technically before tonight. Do you think it will work?" Jared asked her.

Cassie shrugged. She really had no clue.

"How long before the stuff tonight?"

Jared glanced at the clock next to the bed.

"My dad likes to do things at one in the morning, so we have at least six hours before we have to head there," Jared replied.

Cassie nodded. She wasn't sure how long it would last, but she did have the backup vial to break the bond if she needed to a second time.

"That should work, hopefully."

Jared nodded to Cassie and then turned to Nate.

"I know this is awkward and all, so could you like go take a walk while we do this?"

Nate's ears perked up. They didn't know how he would leave, but he had the perfect out now.

"How long do you want him gone?" Cassie asked.

"Forever?" Jared tried.

Raising his lips, Nate bared his teeth with a growl at Jared. *'Not going to happen.'*

"As you can see, the answer is no," Cassie replied a bit more diplomatically.

"Well, we leave for the ceremony in six hours or so. Can you leave for at least four hours?" Jared asked.

Nate pretended to think about it.

'This works out perfectly for you to get out of here without any suspicion,' Cassie replied.

'Yes, but I'm still worried,' Nate stated. *'Promise me you won't leave his side for any reason, even if it means just going upstairs. Don't allow yourself to be alone. It isn't safe here. And you'll do whatever it takes to stay alive in this messed-up place. I have a feeling we can plan all we want,*

but we don't know everything.'

'That's been my life for more than eight years now. I'm used to it,' Cassie replied.

"Does he agree?" Jared asked, assuming they were talking about the time.

"Yes."

Nate's blue tiger eyes stared at Cassie. Everything was messed up.

'I'll be back in four hours to check on you and hopefully, bring a message from your aunt. I'm begging you, for once, listen to me. Don't leave this room if you don't have to. Stay away from all the other wendigo. And don't forget that I love you.'

Cassie watched out the window as Nate disappeared into the trees in the setting sunlight. She thought she saw him turn back once, but he said nothing across the bond. He could feel how difficult it was for Cassie.

She returned to the futon in Jared's room and sat down in front of the vial.

Everything was getting more and more messed up. She thought she didn't want to be with Nate, but now he made her stomach flutter just by looking at her. Then there was Jared. She really didn't know him, but with her memories now back, she could vividly remember what their future could have been like. In that lifetime, she would have loved him and loved him greatly. Everything about him was familiar, so natural. Boys and love were all new to her, and to throw that on top of all the new night human stuff was just all overwhelming. She needed things to slow down so that she could figure out what she wanted instead of life moving so fast that she couldn't catch up.

"Do you need to drink it all, or can we save some in case it wears off before the ceremony?" Jared asked exactly what she had been thinking.

"I think a few drops will make it work. I was thinking of drinking half, just to be on the safe side," Cassie replied.

She stared at the vial in front of her, making no movement to grab it. She had already done the bond thing once. It was intense, and she was just getting used to being bonded to Nate after a week of having him in her head. She wasn't exactly ready to do that again. And breaking the bond was worse. Now that he was there, she was kind of worried about not having that connection. What if her aunt needed her help? What if he needed to speak to her?

Jared sat beside Cassie, startling her from her thoughts.

"I thought it would be less awkward if Nate wasn't around, but I can see that didn't change much," Jared told her. "I was serious in that I don't want to make you do something you don't want to do. I know Nate did that to you already. I'm not like him and never have been."

Cassie couldn't help the giggle that escaped. They were more alike than different.

Jared shook his head. "Okay, I'm not like Nate in that matter. We don't have to do this right now. We can wait until later, right before Nate comes back," Jared suggested.

Reaching forward, she grabbed the bottle. They could wait, but it wouldn't make a difference. It still had to be done. She uncorked the vial and tipped it back, trying not to gag on the horrible taste. She really needed to work on that.

The bond instantly snapped. Cassie felt it disappear when she went to Turner's town, but now it actually felt like it was cut. Cassie grabbed her stomach in the pain of it. She felt like vomiting right there. Jared pulled her into his arms, but the pain was still there.

"Cas, open up your mouth," Jared instructed while her eyes were clenched shut. She did and squinted at him in the light, which was twice as bright as she thought it just was.

Jared raised his wrist and turned from her. When he turned back, blood was dripping down his arm from biting it. Cassie hoped his blood was healing her like Nate's had when she was attacked. She needed relief because the pain wasn't going away … it was getting worse. She opened her mouth, and he pressed his wrist to her lips. After taking only one lick, she felt the burn of the blood as she swallowed it. It felt like drinking a magic-laced drink, but somehow different. It was warmer and eased the pain where much of magic tasted bitter and horrible.

The pain dulled, but it was still there. The pain had to mean something. Maybe she shouldn't have broken the bond. Cassie didn't have time to ponder that as Jared held her face still so that he could look into her eyes.

"It's not gone, is it?" he asked about the pain.

Cassie couldn't verbally reply as she was afraid if she opened her mouth she would puke.

Jared tenderly picked up her wrist. He looked at Cassie, and she knew what he planned to do. Squeezing her eyes shut, she waited. She felt pressure on her wrist but no pain. She was going to open her eyes to see why he was waiting when she felt him in her mind. She kept her eyes shut now as he was still partially transformed. She didn't need to see Jared as one of the monsters from her dreams. She wanted to keep him in her mind as the stunning spotted black leopard instead of the red-eyed monster of her dreams.

"Cas, I'm not that monster anymore," Jared said as he stroked her cheek.

Cassie slowly opened her eyes. The lights were back to normal, and the pain in her stomach was completely gone.

Jared sat next to her on the couch, but he didn't look anything the same. While the wendigo were grotesque-shaped with long, clawed arms, legs that were bent for maximum speed, and razor-sharp teeth set into an animal-like face with beady red-glowing eyes, Jared was nothing like that. Cassie reached forward and touched his furry face. He wasn't the black she remembered, but his features were now more cat and human mixed in a pale white color. The spots were a light gray on his exposed arms. He was larger, not quite twice his normal size, but large enough to make Cassie feel tiny next to him.

"Is this really you?" Cassie asked in awe. He was kind of beautiful in a weird monster way.

"This is what we're supposed to look like," Jared explained, covering her hand on his face with his own.

"No, you're supposed to be a big black cat," Cassie corrected.

Wendigo Jared smiled. His sharp, fanged teeth were still there along with the razor-sharp claws on his fingers, but he looked much more human. The short, fuzzy hair that covered him was soft to the touch, and the best part was that his eyes were back to his normal brown color.

Rising, Cassie walked around him. His shirt was in pieces as he grew in size, and she saw his full back. A raised white line ran the length of his back and a black tattoo like Nate's covered over it on both sides. Cassie had seen Nate's marking only a couple of times. Jared's was different in shape, but not size.

"Do you feel better?" Jared asked. His voice was different as it resonated a bit deeper than his normal voice.

"Yes," she answered as she touched the long scar. She didn't need to ask what it was from. That was where the last bit of his leopard was ripped from him.

Cassie walked back around in front of him.

"Does it feel different?" she asked. He looked different, but she was unsure why that mattered. He still wasn't close to passing for human. This form was still scary to anyone outside the night human world.

Jared nodded as he stood and stretched his arms and flexed his muscles.

"I can feel the strength my father always talks about. Yes. It's much different." His arms almost touched the ceiling. Jared rolled his head around. "And something else. It just feels different. Like I can feel all the wendigo better than before."

Jared flexed his arms one last time before changing back into his normal self. He sat down next to Cassie, shirtless as his was now in shreds.

"Do you really feel better?" he asked, searching her eyes for the truth.

"Yes. I broke the bond for someone else, and he never said it felt horrible," Cassie explained. "I wasn't expecting that."

Jared nodded. "Do you want to rest a little before we have to head out?"

Cassie glanced at the window. It was getting darker out, and a one o'clock meeting meant no nighttime sleep.

"Sure," she replied, standing to head back upstairs. She walked toward the doorway, but stopped. Nate's begging popped into her head. She promised to not go upstairs alone.

"What's wrong?" Jared asked, jumping to her side before she could say anything.

"Nate said I shouldn't leave your side for any reason," Cassie admitted.

"But you still need to rest," Jared replied. "Come on."

Taking her hand in his, he led her upstairs. She felt a warm hum when his hand touched hers. It felt normal, like she had held his hand a hundred times already. It made Jared happy, but Cassie didn't know what to think. Jared smiled as she thought that.

"Are you inside my head?" she asked. Nate had been kind enough to stay out, or if he did see something, he kept it to himself.

"I'm not trying. It kind of goes with the whole mate thing," Jared replied. "Just like you knew I was happy before I smiled."

Her brow furrowed, not realizing she had done that. "Fine," she muttered, giving and not continuing to pout about it.

Jared walked into the room and dropped Cassie's hand as she reached the bed.

"You rest, and I'll just sit over there." Jared pointed to the chair next to the windows.

"You'll wake me when Nate comes back?" Cassie asked.

"Yes. Now get some rest."

Cassie climbed into the large king-sized bed. The covers were cold, and she shivered—not knowing if it was from the cold or from being alone. The large bed just emphasized that she was all alone now, just like the bond with Nate being gone left her without the clan or the coven. The bed bounced, and Cassie opened her eyes to find Jared lying behind her. He wrapped his arms around her, keeping her tucked tightly into the covers. She could feel his warmness through them.

"You aren't alone, Cassie, and never will be," Jared whispered into her ear before gently kissing her cheek. "Now rest."

CHAPTER 9

The knock at the door wasn't loud enough to normally wake Cassie, but now she felt things through her new mate as well. The soft pounding from the room below was enough to make him move. Cassie could sense it was a wendigo at the door, and that Jared already knew it was his brother. How he knew was beyond Cassie, but she hurried off the bed to follow him downstairs, no matter how sleepy she still was.

Cassie plopped down on the futon as Jared answered the door.

"We have a bit of an issue," Ryder whispered to his brother.

Jared shrugged. "You're going to have to get used to telling us both stuff. She's my mate and soon enough will be able to hear every thought I think."

'Like why in the world did he have to wake us when we both were comfortably asleep?' Jared said to Cassie.

She covered her laugh with a fake cough.

"I didn't think she'd like to hear this one, and you might want to take care of it yourself," Ryder cryptically explained before sending a bunch of images to Jared. Cassie caught bits of them as it was the first time she ever felt Jared's bond to his clan.

"Cassie, we need to go take care of this," Jared told her.

Jared slowed the images down because she was confused. Nate was in a cage and lashing out at anyone who came near. They had tased him as he was walking through the woods and caged him.

Ryder watched as she stood and took Jared's outstretched

hand.

"Father was worried that after you guys bonded in a couple hours it would break the hold Cassie has on Nate, and he will go feral like the rest of the skinwalkers," Ryder explained, leading them outside.

Cassie hadn't even thought of that. She had never once, even before she was bonded to Nate, feared his tiger. And she was pretty certain not all were feral, but she kept that to herself and hoped Jared didn't see that thought.

"You don't have to cage him," Cassie stated as Ryder opened the door.

'We don't know that,' Jared answered. *'We didn't even think about what it would do to break the bond with him.'*

Cassie already felt bad about that. She hadn't thought about the pain because she didn't know. Did Nate go through that pain? Was he really feral?

Ryder led them to the barn where his truck was parked outside … just like when Cassie first woke up with the wendigo, except this time Whitney wasn't in the cage, but Nate was. A couple of the night humans hanging around were jeering at Nate in the cage. He sat perfectly still until they got close enough for him to lash out at them. He wasn't even close to being feral. He was his normal, calculated self. And if she wasn't bonded to him, Nate was still marked as her mate. She could very faintly feel his emotions, and he was ticked off.

Cassie walked over to the cage and Nate immediately sat down nicely.

"Let him out of there," she ordered Ryder.

Ryder looked to Jared, and Jared shrugged his reply.

'Is that really the best idea?' Jared asked.

Cassie turned to him. *'What proof do you need?'* she asked. *'I know he's still in there. I can see it in his eyes. The mating bond didn't disappear. He's stable even if he's just a tiger now.'*

Jared didn't appear convinced.

Cassie looked over to Nate.

"Nate, can you prove to Jared that you are safe to let go?" Cassie asked out loud for everyone.

Tiger Nate rolled his eyes before standing up as much as he could in the cramped cage and pushing forward against the bars to allow Cassie to pet him. She ran her hand down his striped fur, and he turned to lick her hand.

"He's perfectly safe, but if you guys think he'll be a problem, I can send him away," Cassie suggested. The other wendigo seemed to like that idea, but Ryder was still waiting for Jared to tell him what to do.

Jared nodded. "We can walk him to the edge of the property and send him on his way."

'Thank you,' Cassie replied.

Ryder unlocked the cage, and Nate jumped out of it in one graceful leap that landed him on the ground next to Cassie. Tiger Nate rubbed his head under her hand. The nearest wendigo that had been harassing him backed slowly away as Nate raised his lips to show off his teeth with a soft growl. Cassie batted his head.

"Knock that off," she scolded him. Nate turned to her and licked her hand. It had been hard to see him walk away and even harder to break the bond, but Nate was acting like good old Nate. "And knock that off, too. Tiger licks are gross and very wet."

Nate seemed to huff a laugh, his tongue hanging out to get her another time.

"This way," Jared directed Cassie and Nate as they began to walk away from the house.

Jared stayed on alert. Cassie could sense that he didn't think Nate was actually in full control. He was anxious to get him off the wendigo land and away from Cassie. He led the way in the dark night and had to occasionally help Cassie not trip on anything. Cassie laughed at the one time where both the guys had to make sure she didn't fall down. She was the only one hiking in the dark without night vision. As Jared slowed down, Cassie saw Nate pause.

"Once he passes those two trees he'll be outside the perimeter to our clan. None of the wendigo have permission to hunt outside our grounds. You will be safe there," Jared explained. "But if you come back, I can't guarantee you won't be killed next time. Many are very afraid of you, and my father would rather not have a single living skinwalker around. Releasing them is what I bargained for. That doesn't mean he will respect that if you come back. You've already seen how much patience he has."

Nate turned back to Cassie. In his tiger body on four legs he basically stood eye-to-eye with her. Nate turned his glowing blue eyes to Cassie and waited. Cassie smiled; she knew what he wanted. Placing a hand on his head, Cassie peered into his eyes. It would only be a one-way conversation, but it was better than nothing.

Cassie watched her aunt speak to her through Nate's eyes. *'Hi, Cassie. Nate found us and filled us in on everything. We are pretty sure we know where they're keeping the witches. They have a sacred ground they do all their ceremonies on. We found it the first day we went looking. Underneath the ground are all sorts of caves. Nate's been able to contact his dad, and he's helping us find the witches by finding his mother. We plan to get them tonight while the wendigo are distracted by your ceremony. You are our distraction. The younger skinwalkers are all following Nate's commands and will attack if we need more time to get everyone out. They have been warned to stay away from Jared as it will hurt you, too. Please stay safe and we will on our end. Nate will come for you once everyone is out and to safety.'*

Cassie rubbed Nate's head. It was strange to not hear him. She could remember the first few nights when she thought Nate was Whitney. She told him she wished he could be a talking tiger. Again, she wanted that. It was too quiet without a response from him.

"Tell her I miss her," Cassie said quietly. "Was it painful for you, too?" She had to ask.

Nate cocked his head to the side as if he didn't understand.

"When the bond broke," Cassie added. Nate shook his head. "Good." That didn't explain anything, but at least she didn't hurt him by doing it.

Nate peered around Cassie to Jared, who was waiting back a few feet, giving them space.

"He's been fine. Don't worry. It worked, and his father will have nothing to be upset about."

Cassie reached out for Nate again but pulled her hand back. She could feel through the bond that there were many wendigo in the woods. They were growing impatient, and they all were looking at Nate as a meal.

"You really should get going. These guys don't seem too patient, and I'm pretty sure there are several waiting for you to not leave," Cassie added what she felt through the bond with Jared. Several was an understatement. It was closer to a couple dozen, but that would make Nate stay instead of leave.

Nate glanced back at Jared one more time.

Jared came closer and put his arm around Cassie's waist.

"She will be safe with me," he promised Nate.

Nate nodded to him and stepped past the boundary. It was as if there was smoke beyond, and he disappeared right into it, vanishing into the night.

"The borders have magic around them," Jared explained. "It helps keep visitors out."

Cassie nodded, staring where Nate had been. She had to hope he stayed safe. They had a plan. She had her part to play, and now she just wanted to go back to Jared's room where she felt safe. Cassie walked holding Jared's hand, and the wendigo, while hidden throughout the woods, walked with them, keeping a silent watch over the two of them.

'They are here to protect us,' Jared explained. *'My father*

has been bugging me for years to join him as a full wendigo; I have a feeling he's afraid something will happen now that I have you.'

'It does that seem to work way, doesn't it?' Cassie replied, still uneasy with the monsters around her.

Smiling, Jared shook his head. *'I know why you think we are monsters, but more than half the men here aren't here by their choice. There are a lot of people that get kicked out of the skinwalker clan. They had no place to go and chose to join us.'*

'But I sense so much evil around here,' Cassie commented. Evil seeped from the ground they were walking on.

'The evil comes from the other half of the wendigo. Ones born here and those that want to rise in power tend to do very bad things. There are two ways to become a full wendigo. You find a mate to balance your power, or you drain a witch,' Jared explained. *'The men following us around chose not to drain a witch, and remain in their pledge stages. There are some good men here. I promise you.'*

'And your brother?' Cassie asked, remembering the red-eyed monster that stared at her like she was its favorite snack.

'Doesn't know what he wants to be yet,' Jared answered as they made their way back to the clearing by the barn.

Jared paused as they walked into the open. The moon was shining bright, and Cassie saw the way back to the house. Lights were on in various rooms, but there was one without a light. She didn't need to see the silhouette in the window to know they were being watched. She could feel it through Jared.

'My father doubts that we will bond,' Jared explained the feelings Cassie could feel.

'And he thinks a love potion will do the trick?' she asked, seeing if her train of thought was right.

Jared's father was a lot more observant than the rest of the wendigo and that worried Cassie. Nate had warned her that he was smart and cunning. She didn't want him forcing Jared to look deeper into the thoughts she was trying to keep away from them.

'Then I guess you better kiss me,' Cassie replied.

Jared seemed momentarily shocked, but easily turned to her and pulled her close enough to kiss. Tilting her head back, she held onto the front of his shirt. He leaned down and met her halfway, and when his lips touched her, it made her stomach flutter. In the future she had seen, she had kissed him hundreds of times in secret. She remembered exactly how it felt, and it felt just as perfect now. There was something about Jared that was different than Nate. He didn't kiss her with a desperation that she was leaving, but with the confidence she was already his. Pulling back, Jared smiled at her.

'We still have an audience?'

'Yep,' he answered, and took her back to the house.

As they neared, Cassie could feel Ben through the bond. He was still in the house watching them as they entered. Jared turned and led her through the house to his bedroom. The evil presence followed them as they walked. Cassie kept her hand in Jared's hand even though she wanted to run to his room as quickly as possible. Ben following them made her uneasy. So far he had been indifferent to whether they bonded or Jared killed her. She just didn't want him to change his mind and decide she was more useful dead.

Opening his room door, Jared let Cassie in and shut the door without looking behind. Neither of them needed to see to know that his father was still stalking them.

'He's right outside the door now,' he explained.

The barrier Cassie put up dulled her sense of him near. The bond was enough to show her Jared was right. Ben was standing just outside the doorway.

'What is he waiting for?' Cassie asked.

Jared shrugged. *'My guess? He didn't believe our kiss outside.'*

'Fine,' Cassie replied, grabbing both of Jared's hands and pulling him across the room.

Jared wasn't expecting Cassie to do that and tripped, causing her to giggle.

"Not so graceful all the time I see," Cassie teased.

Jared swept her into his arms. "You better hope I'm graceful now, or we both fall down."

Cassie giggled more as Jared marched over to his bed, where he pretended to trip and dump her on it. She tried to roll out of the way when he fake fell to the bed, but instead got trapped beneath him.

"Hey, I'm stuck," Cassie teased.

"Guess you need to pay me to get me to move," he teased back.

'Still there?' she asked.

'Yep.'

Cassie pushed up enough on her elbows for her lips to reach him. He was only momentarily shocked as he began to kiss her back. She could still feel Ben outside the room. What more would convince him? She needed to be more convincing but had no idea how to do so. She had never even had a boyfriend, and Jared was only the second guy she kissed, ever.

Pulling back, Jared gazed into her eyes. If she wanted, he was being an open book. The bond gave her access to his memories, but it was something different now. He was offering his past to her. He was offering everything to her.

Cassie took a deep breath. She had seen the future. She didn't have real experience with boys, but her future would have been very different if someone hadn't changed it all. She would have spent more time alone with him than anyone approved of. She would have been in love with Jared. Cassie thought of that future she saw and reached up to pull his face closer. She didn't need to see his past now. She needed to remember what should have been.

Jared's lips met hers, this time ready for her. She didn't think as her hands roamed down his chest and began to undo each button of his shirt. When the last button was undone, Jared stood back up and silently crept to the closed door.

'He's gone. That round was convincing enough,' Jared told her silently.

Cassie nodded. She'd go with that. She didn't want to admit the real truth to him. For a brief moment, she forgot she was supposed to be convincing Ben that they were deeply in love. She was living in the memory of a future which would never happen. She wasn't playing a part; she was feeling the emotion hidden in her heart.

An hour passed and Ben didn't return. Jared and Cassie stayed near each other in the room in case he did, but he didn't. Time passed slowly as Cassie watched Jared. She really knew nothing about him now. He was as much a stranger as Nate, yet somehow she was still connected to him. Kissing him felt as perfect as it did with Nate, and Jared was a lot more empathetic to her not wanting to be bonded to anyone. She wanted to be free to make her own choice, no matter how right it felt with either guy. She was worried the bonds would confuse her. Maybe she wouldn't have felt anything if they hadn't forced her to be their mates. Okay, that wasn't true. She'd had a crush on Nate for years. And Jared had filled in her memories now.

Jared spent time on his phone and then his computer. Cassie didn't dare turn on the TV in case that dulled the sound of Ben returning. She didn't have much to do beyond think.

Was it bad that the coven was gone now? They were trying to force her to bind to Nate, and they wanted to drain all her witch powers as it sounded like they did to her mother. Without the coven, her life would have been much different. Then again, if she had the future she saw as a kid, her life would have been different also. All Cassie could figure was her life was supposed to be different. But that didn't matter now. She needed to figure out what she wanted from her life at the moment and go with it. She had two great guys that wanted her in two completely different night human worlds. Their short term plan looked like it was working, but that was just it. It was a short term plan.

Jared glanced up from his phone. Cassie didn't know if he was looking in on her thoughts. At this point, she kind of didn't care. It wasn't like she was hiding the fact that she was confused and wanted the world to freeze and let her off the crazy night human train.

"We should probably get ready to go. My dad likes to start everything at one, but we might want to go scope it out beforehand. Your cousin didn't like my protest against binding you to everyone, and he left a bit easier than I expected," Jared explained, finally talking.

"In that case, give me a minute here." Cassie went to the kit and pulled out some ingredients. She hadn't thought of it before, but there was one thing she could do.

She didn't need much time to make a counter magic spell. It was easier than something from scratch. All they really had time for or needed was to make anything Jack tried to bounce off them. Cassie mixed the plants and squished the liquid from the leaves.

"Come here," Cassie said to Jared, who had been watching her out of the corner of his eye.

Jared walked over and stood in front of Cassie. She could feel the curiosity coming off him and through the bond, but she ignored it, just like she ignored the feeling of wanting to kiss him. She knew how the bond worked, and it played with her emotions. It was a mating bond after all, but Cassie had no intention of *mating* with anyone.

"Down here." Cassie waved for him to bend down while she still held onto the mortar and moved the pestle out of the way.

Jared leaned down. Cassie dipped her fingers in the green goo and then dabbed it on his head. She added a bit of her own magic into the mixture.

"And this would be?" Jared asked, trying to look at his forehead.

"I like to call it my 'I'm rubber, you're glue' mix. Whit and I figured this one out years ago to get through high school. It's a reflection spell. It basically throws back at the spell caster what they just did. It only works once, so if something goes down, we'll have to act from there," Cassie explained.

"One chance, huh?" Jared asked, not touching it.

"Hey, that's better than nothing."

She still wished she knew how those sidhe magic users fought so easily, throwing magic out of their fingertips. It would have been helpful. She was going to have to make a note to call Devin some time and ask him or Nessa. They owed her that much, she hoped.

"Hey. I wasn't knocking it. It's more than I'm contributing." Jared surrendered with his hands in the air. "Actually, after you go look upstairs at what you get to wear to the meeting tonight, you might regret sharing that with me."

Cassie opened her eyes and was about to ask what he meant, but Jared pushed her before she could. "Upstairs."

Jared went into the large walk-in closet in the room and pulled out a white bag just like the one Whitney had brought their homecoming dresses into school just weeks ago. After placing the bag on the bed, he backed up. Cassie looked at him, and he motioned for her to open it. How bad could it be? Whitney brought her essentially a shirt to wear to a dance. What could the wendigo want her to wear?

Cassie unzipped the bag. Deep purple fluff came out of the bag like it had been packed tightly. Cassie looked up to Jared. There was a lot more poof to the dress than the last one she wore.

"Not me. This is all my father. He kind of has this thing about wanting the ceremonies to be all fancy," Jared explained.

"Then where's your tux?" Cassie asked in reply.

Jared kind of shook his head. "Let me rephrase that. My father wants any women presented in front of the clan to be all fancy. If you couldn't tell, we don't have too many women around, and my father likes the ones we do to be dressed up."

Cassie nodded. "Double standards."

Jared nodded with her. "Yep. Double standards. Not my say, though. I'd rather much more of you be covered up. With your neck exposed, you'll be a tempting meal for anyone there."

She pulled the dress free from the bag and held it up by the hanger. The almost black dress was a full-length ball gown. The top was jeweled from the almost strapless top that was held by the thinnest spaghetti straps, down past the hips where all the extra material flared from. The dress wasn't close to Cassie's style, and the floor-length skirt seemed a bit counterproductive since Jared was expecting a fight.

"Where exactly are we going for this tonight?" Cassie asked, hoping they only had to go downstairs to the grand dining room. Her aunt said something about a ritual space in the woods. The dress wasn't for hiking.

"The woods." Jared tried to look away as he talked.

"The woods?" Cassie asked as if she heard wrong. *Who would take a girl out into the woods in a dress like that? Is he serious?* she thought.

"We have a stone outcrop that we use when we deal with the full clan," Jared explained.

"The full clan?" Cassie asked. She was glad she was getting more details, but wasn't sure she really wanted to hear them. When he said she would be a tempting meal, she was imagining for a few wendigo. She had no clue how big a full clan would be.

Jared shrugged. "Me becoming a full wendigo means that I'll move into the spot as my father's second-in-command. I become the beta to my father the alpha. It's kind of a big deal." Jared rubbed his head, pulling back his brown locks. He seemed embarrassed by it all.

Cassie rubbed her forehead. Life just couldn't be easy for her.

"I wear this dress to go for a walk through the woods to some stones, to meet with the whole clan that will view me as a meal? Didn't your father say something about witch blood being enticing? Is this safe? How the heck do I run away in a dress like this?"

Cassie wasn't looking forward to all of it anyway, but the wendigo still scared her. She saw them every night in her dreams. Their red eyes haunted every moment her eyes closed for the past week, except for when Jared was holding her. The bonding thing was getting less and less inviting than it already was, and that was hard to do since bonding to another night human in front of a bunch of hungry, scary night humans was the last thing she wanted to do.

"Cassie, I will never let anything happen to you," Jared told her solemnly, picking up on her fears.

"Let? I don't doubt you would try to keep me safe, but let's be real. I've seen enough in the past two weeks to know that we have very little control over anything."

Jared stopped looking at the dress and picked up her hand.

"As long as I'm breathing, you'll be safe. No one will harm you before or after this ceremony."

Cassie gave him a weak smile. She used to be optimistic like him, but that had changed. She now lived in the real world and knew what was waiting for her. Jared was honestly pledging his life to her and because of the bond, there wasn't much they could do that didn't involve the other, but that still didn't mean things would easily go their way. Cassie had felt Jared's father at the doorway through the bond. He was making sure his son was really going to bond with Cassie, but she felt something else. He wasn't just being the nice, doting father. There was something behind him that she couldn't put her finger on. Ben was just one more mystery for her, one that scared the crap out of her. When she looked in his eyes, she only saw evil. Jared's pledge was nice, but Cassie knew they had less control than he realized.

CHAPTER 10

"**You're not serious**," Cassie complained for the second time.

She was standing outside in the cool night air in nothing more than a spaghetti-strapped prom dress. Jared had just explained it would be quickest for her to let him carry her to the meeting place because it was far away.

"When you said in the woods, I don't know, I kind of pictured taking a car somewhere and getting out close by," Cassie complained.

She really didn't want to be in the thick of the woods at nighttime to begin with, but Jared taking her meant she had no chance to know where she was going or how to get back to the safe room she had created with her spell.

Jared didn't wait for her to agree as he scooped her into his arms.

"I can take you, or we can go find Jack. I'm sure he would be more than willing to flash you over there, but you'll either have to wait here or there for me to catch up."

Cassie pouted. She really didn't want to wander around the wood in a prom dress or without shoes. That was the kicker of it all—they expected her to stand around the woods without shoes. She kind of got the sense that was planned to keep her from running, but she wasn't about to say that out loud. Jared was already embarrassed by the weirdness of all of it.

"It works best if you keep your eyes closed. Otherwise you might get a little motion sick," Jared explained.

"I know. Not my first time carried through the woods like

a sack of potatoes. Whitney's carried me around before." Cassie added the last part as she felt the jealousy rise in him when she mentioned it wasn't her first time. "She, at least, lets me stay warm."

Cassie tucked her arms into the light coat Jared was wearing and huddled against his bare chest. It seemed his clothing choice was made for him and included only a pair of elastic waist pants that would be too short when he finally transformed.

"See, not so bad," Jared commented, obviously enjoying the snuggled together position.

"Speak for yourself, buddy," Cassie replied. Jared mocked being hurt since he could feel her emotions just as she could feel his across the bond. "You're not being dragged off into the woods in a ball gown and no shoes."

"Hey, half naked here. Not much better off. No shoes either." Jared picked up a foot, wiggling his toes for her to see.

He had her there. He wasn't in any better clothing position, but at least he didn't care about the cold. Normally Cassie didn't mind the cold either. She loved the winter and the few snow storms that came with it, but while her nerves were becoming unraveled, she didn't need the cold to remind her how messed up everything was.

"Ready?" Jared asked, glancing down at her in his arms.

"Do I have a choice?"

"Neither of us does," Jared answered with the truth of the matter.

His father's order was bothering him. He wanted nothing more than to make his own choices and not have his life dictated to him. His father walked a fine line with Jared. Ben knew enough to back off every now and then and pretend like Jared had an option, but Cassie could see it through Jared's memories that he had no option in anything. His father was grooming him into his second-in-command, and there was no out for Jared. She knew that feeling all too well. She had yet to find a way out herself.

Jared began with a couple of slow steps before picking up speed. Closing her eyes, she pressed her face into his chest. Jared laughed as he ran faster. If she opened her eyes, she would see nothing. When Nate attacked him the day before, she had seen that Jared moved almost as fast as the wind.

The bond was clear to Cassie as she pressed against him. He was enjoying his run and actually considered slowing down to have a few more seconds. His feelings were loud and clear. He was in love with her and had been since they were children. Had their lives turned out as they were supposed to, Cassie would have been in love with him, too. But her life wasn't that way. Part of her tried to convince the rest of her that she remembered him. In reality, she knew Jared even less than Nate. At least, she had seen Nate five days a week for the past eight years as they went to school together. Jared was still a mystery she was learning more about.

'You know I didn't want it to be this way,' Jared told her through the bond as the wind whipped past her face, making it impossible to hear anything.

'I know,' Cassie replied. And she did know. He was completely serious about not forcing her into anything, and as far as she saw it, he wasn't. His father was the one forcing her.

Jared slowed down.

'Here already?' she asked.

'Close enough.'

Cassie slowly opened her eyes and adjusted to the moonlight that lit the woods around her. There was enough light to see dimly, but she had nowhere near the sight of Jared. He didn't seem to even notice the dark around them. Jared moved to set her down, and Cassie clung to his neck.

'No shoes, remember?'

Jared held her and scooped her back up. *'Sorry. I forgot. I never wear shoes anymore. I'm always transforming and wrecking them, so I just stopped wearing them.'*

'Well, no super monster feet here, even if I come from night humans,' Cassie added, readjusting her arms inside Jared's coat. She wasn't looking forward to the cool air when he finally did have to set her down.

Cassie saw the bodies standing around before she saw the stones. Several stones—at least ten feet high—jutted out of the ground. The men who were waiting around stood amongst them, facing what Cassie had to assume was the center as she could see faces in the distance between the men whose backs she saw. As they neared the men, the ones she saw were on the outer edge. There was a ring of men standing shoulder-to-shoulder with a large empty space in the middle—at least thirty feet in diameter. There were flat stones where all the men stood, and Cassie saw that she wouldn't need shoes at all.

Jared gently set Cassie down behind the men.

'Do you feel any magic?' Jared asked.

Cassie closed her eyes and took a deep breath.

'Yes. Someone created a casting circle of power with the men of the circle inside it,' Cassie explained.

'And what can we do about it?' Jared helped her with her potions before, but now that she could see inside his head, it was more of a physical help because he knew nothing of magic.

'Where is your father?'

'Standing directly north,' Jared replied. It was his spot at every function.

'Can we come in on the south side, directly across from him?'

Jared took her hand and walked her around the circle clockwise from where he had set her down. He stopped outside the men, and she looked at the ground. There, behind the men who formed the inner circle, was a stone with magic etched into it.

'Do you see that stone?' Cassie sent Jared a picture in her

mind.

'Yes,' he replied.

'That writing needs to be scraped off and then the spell will be incomplete. It would be even better to hit all four ordinals to the circle, but just one should weaken it enough to make whatever he had planned not work,' Cassie explained.

'Where should the other ones be?'

'I can't tell from here,' she replied.

'Could you tell from inside the circle?'

'Yes, but you wouldn't be able to pay me to cross the line while those are intact. I have no idea what my cousin can do.'

'Or your uncle,' Jared added, looking around. *'Do you trust me?'*

That was a loaded question. Did she trust him? The old Jared, her friend, growing up? She trusted him. Wendigo Jared she kind of trusted, but not the same. Right now? She wanted to trust him, but he had to do whatever his father told him. It was hard to trust with that.

Reaching down, Jared threaded his fingers through hers and held her hand.

'No. I don't follow his rule now. He's the alpha, but you come first. We are bonded. He can't make me do anything to hurt you because it would hurt myself,' Jared explained, not minding that she just mentally admitted she didn't trust him.

Cassie took a deep breath. Jared was looking for her trust.

'Gonna fill me in on what's coming next, or do I just wing it?' There wasn't much more she could do. The spell was etched in stone.

'Nope. Just let your mate take care of all this,' Jared replied and gave her a wink.

Jared led Cassie up to the south side of the circle. She felt the magic pulsing off the circle and really didn't want to know what spell was cast there. Her reflection spell would only give them one chance, and it probably wasn't best to use her trump card at the beginning of the night. Jared paused as he stood on the stone with the symbol etched into it. She could feel inside him as something switched. It wasn't until she heard the scratching at their feet before she looked down to see his long sharp claws running across the symbol. The power behind the circle cast melted away.

'Guess that will do,' Cassie replied.

'Not quite. I don't like taking chances, so I will let you go in the middle and make my way around to the other ones before we do this.' Jared leaned down and kissed her forehead.

"I'll meet you in there," he promised out loud.

The men standing inside the now defunct circle moved out of the way to let Cassie pass.

Jared kept behind the circle while urging her forward. Taking a deep breath and holding her head high, she entered the ring of men, at least they were still in the form of men, but she knew each person there was really a wendigo. She preferred they stay as men.

Jared walked around the circle slowly, breaking it along the way.

'Where is the west one?' Jared asked. Cassie was happy to not have to look at the wooden post she was approaching and turned to watch him instead.

'The blond-haired guy, two more ahead.'

Jared paused and scraped his nails across that rock, too, destroying the second spell that had been placed.

'The north one is behind your father,' Cassie added.

He didn't head that way, but turned and walked back the way they came.

'East one?'

'Behind the guy that looks like he's ready to transform,' Cassie added as Jared neared the man. His eyes kept flashing to red, like he had no control over the beast inside of him.

Jared scratched out the stone before going behind his father to do the same. Cassie stopped walking to the center of the circle. A large, almost completely circular stone made up the center of the circle of men. Cassie didn't want to even touch it. She could feel the evil coming off it and the blood which had been shed. Hundreds of people had died there. Glancing at the post protruding out of the middle of the stone, she saw that chains and a rope hung from it. Jared finished scraping out the spell and messing up the circle of power. It was safe for them to be inside it now. Jared moved to his father's right side while Ryder stood at his left.

"Grand entrance as always, Son," Ben said more than loud enough for everyone to hear. A couple of the men in the circle chuckled.

Jared gave him a grim smile as he looked to Cassie standing in the middle of the circle.

Ben waved his hand. "Go to her; you won't be any fun until you're with her."

He spoke like it was a big, friendly meeting; not a bunch of blood hungry monsters who were standing around licking their lips like they would be getting a taste of Cassie soon. She was more than happy to take Jared's outstretched hand. Moving behind her, he wrapped his protective arms around her waist.

"I take it you still want to bond instead of feed on her?" Ben asked, and a few more of the men chuckled.

"That's never been a question," Jared responded seriously, even if his father was joking or not.

Ben shrugged. "Oh, well. What can I do? I raised him to be strong and independent, and this is what I get. Fine. Get the show done so we can move on with other details."

He acted like he was bored, but his eyes said otherwise. He still was assessing Cassie and making a decision about her. Jared turned Cassie in his arms so that her back was to his father, then lowered his head to her and placed his nose tip to tip with her own. His large brown eyes stared at her.

Jared's memory flowed from him to Cassie. They were young, maybe six or seven, and Nate was home sick. Cassie and Jared were alone and ran around the park on their own while John was sleeping on a bench. Jared had asked John to watch them because he hoped he would fall asleep. It was fall after all. Cassie and Jared had just barricaded themselves under one of the slides with the sand piled all the way up to the steps. Beyond their feet, no one would have been able to guess where they were. The space was small, and if alone, one would have been able to hide, but together, they were squished into it. Cassie and Jared had been having much fun under the steps as they never could fit all three of them under it.

'That was the first time I realized I didn't want to share you with Nate. I didn't want to have to share you with anyone. That was the day I realized that maybe I wanted you to be more than just my friend,' Jared explained.

Cassie smiled at him. She could see it through his eyes, but with the bond, she felt it also. He had loved her much longer than she knew. Cassie hated that her memories had been taken from her, but even more so that she could have ever forgotten Jared. He was as much a part of her childhood as anything else.

'Ready to act your heart out?' Jared asked.

'Hey, you're the one that has to do the acting. I just need to play along,' Cassie reminded him.

Jared pulled his head back.

"Should we tie her up?" one of the older wendigo asked, licking his lips.

"Yeah, she looks like she might be a fainter," another one added.

Jared ignored them, and Cassie tried to do the same. It was much harder to ignore Ben's presence behind her, though. He was staring intently, and even without looking at him, Cassie could get a feeling from him. He was anxious and starting to doubt Jared and Cassie again. Even Jared had noticed.

After pulling a pocket knife out of his pants, Jared flicked it open and handed it to Cassie blade side away from her. Staring at him, she took it.

"Um, yeah." She wasn't exactly sure what she was supposed to do. They had been planning what to do if something went wrong, but didn't spend any time going over what was supposed to go right.

Jared held out his hand.

"Since I get to feed on you, only fitting you get to make the cut on me," he explained.

'Serious?' Cassie asked across the bond, looking at his hand first and then his eyes. She hadn't even considered that she would be doing that.

'Serious.'

Cassie took his hand in hers. Images flashed before her eyes of the future she had seen. His hands were almost the same, but slightly different. They were the same size and shape, but rougher. His life had been harder this time than it should have been, but she liked the outcome much better. Cassie held the knife above his palm but stopped. She couldn't do it. No matter if it was an eye for an eye, she couldn't cut him.

Smiling, he reached up with his other hand and touched her cheek. "Never could be mean. Glad to see that hasn't changed."

As Jared took his hand away from her face, he put it on top of her hand holding the knife, pressing the blade into his hand. Cassie would have squealed if there weren't many people watching. Jared released her hand then flicked the blade shut. Cassie squeezed her own hand, which had the same cut forming on it.

'Shoot. I didn't think of that,' Jared told her.

'Can you smell it?' Cassie asked. She had been ready for it and kept her hand shut the whole time.

'No. I felt it as it cut you, too,' Jared replied.

Cassie tried to not let out a sigh. Ben was behind her waiting for any reason to swoop in and stop it from happening.

"You first." He held up his bleeding hand for her.

Cassie took his hand and quickly licked the blood off it. The cut on his hand had already closed up, which meant hers was healed as well. She didn't dare unclench her fist, though, in case the dried blood gave it away.

Jared dropped Cassie's hand as he began to move behind her. A few of the men snickered when he did so, but Jared ignored them. He stopped directly behind her and brushed her hair off her neck, exposing the main vein they liked to feed upon. Cassie knew exactly what was coming next.

'It won't hurt,' Jared tried to reassure her.

Cassie turned around in his arms, knowing what she would be facing. "If we are going to do this, we aren't having secrets," she told a shocked Jared.

His shock instantly faded as he gazed into her eyes. She still had nightmares about the wendigo that had hunted her, but she was being brave now. She needed to see that side of him. She needed to be able to let go of the part of her that still looked at him and saw his leopard instead of the wendigo. She needed to see the real Jared.

"You know I have to transform to do this," Jared replied, touching her face gently.

"That's okay."

"But the wendigo scare you," Jared added. "Cas, I know how you feel about us." And he did know. Cassie couldn't hide it from him if she tried, but she didn't try. He could see into her mind now and knew exactly what she went through.

Reaching up with her free hand, she touched his face. Even though she didn't know him like she once did, he was still Jared. Deep inside of him was the same boy that had been her best friend. Deep inside was the young man that would have gone to every length to find a way to be with her. That much of him didn't change.

"Yes, the wendigo scare me, but that's just it. *They* scare me, not you. You could never scare me."

Jared's lips were kissing her before she could even react. Cassie heard chuckles and a few cat-calls around her from the men who were watching. However, the noise around him didn't stop Jared from kissing her. Cassie held onto him when he finally pulled away.

Taking a step back, he slid his hand into hers. The young man with chocolate eyes and dusty brown hair melted into the same monster that haunted Cassie. His body morphed with his legs elongating and popping backward and fur sprouting on him from head-to-toe. His long, sharp-clawed hand still held her, being careful to keep her from the edges of the claws. Cassie looked up into the beady red eyes and didn't even flinch. He was identical to her dreams, but she didn't feel the fear that came with that day. He looked like the monster, but he wasn't the monster. Inside, Jared was still the pure heart that Cassie had grown up with. Jared was still Jared behind the fur.

'You really don't fear me,' Jared said across the bond.

'Because you are still you.'

Cassie flicked her hair back and tilted her neck, knowing exactly what had to come next. The guys around the circle hungrily licked their lips, but Cassie didn't look away from Jared. He slowly leaned down closer to her. She felt his breath upon her neck but didn't flinch. It was Jared after all, no matter how he looked.

Jared was right. Cassie didn't even feel it when he bit into her. She only knew when it happened because she was connected mentally with him. Slowly pulling back, Jared recalled what it felt like only hours ago when he first transformed. Cassie stood still and watched in awe.

His black fur receded as he morphed back into a more human shape. His body bent back into shape while the wolf-like face receded into a cat-like human face. Jared changed slowly and stood up to his now full height. He looked directly at his father and his father nodded to him. All the men around them erupted into cheers.

Ben nodded to Jared when he took Cassie's hand and led her over to the spot in the circle waiting for them. Jared was standing at his father's right hand. Ben patted Jared on the back before taking Cassie's hand in his own, pulling her cut hand loose from her own grasp, keeping it shut.

"Welcome to the family, Cassie."

He turned her hand over where the blood was dried and licked it.

"Go get the main course," Ben called across the circle to the guy standing right near the south stone, which was marked. The men in the circle waited, talking to their neighbors before Ben turned back to Cassie and Jared.

"I don't know how you stopped yourself from draining her. She tastes much better than all the previous witches we've fed upon," Ben commented.

Jared looked to his father. Cassie got the distinct feeling that the *we* Ben used did not include Jared. He had explained more than once that he only drank hospital donated blood, and had never fed on anyone before binding to Cassie.

'You said to bind by tonight. We didn't disobey your orders,' Jared told him mentally.

Ben smiled. *'I didn't mean you had to bind her that way.'*

Jared kept sneaking a peek across the circle where the men behind the circle had parted, and the one that had gone away was making his way back.

'What way?' Cassie asked Jared.

'He thinks we had sex,' Jared replied, keeping his eyes on the people approaching.

'What?' Cassie felt her face turning redder than it ever had. She had been trying to convince Ben she and Jared were in love, but she wasn't thinking of taking it that far.

"I'd love to have a couple dozen grandbabies." Ben chuckled as Cassie turned even redder. "And the sooner, the better. Our clan has gotten smaller over the years."

Cassie would have continued to be mortified, but she finally realized what they were doing across the circle. The man who just left had entered with a girl whose hands were tied in front of her. She had cuts up and down her bare arms, and she was wearing an outfit similar to Cassie's, except it was strapless.

"Help me please," the girl begged each person she passed. "I was trying to get away from the coven. I didn't know this was your land. I'll go away. I promise I'll never come back. I promise."

"Silence," Ben grumbled, and the girl was immediately quiet along with everyone else as his command drifted over them.

The man brought her to the post and tied her arms to the rope that was hanging there before wrapping her foot with the chains. Cassie turned her head into Jared's chest. She could feel the eagerness pour off the men in the circle. They were hungry, and Cassie only had one guess who the meal was.

"Oh, princess. You're going to miss the best part of the night," Ben told Cassie. "Turn her to face this, Jared. She's one of us now, so she better get used to our ways."

Jared paused. His father had given him a command and his hands weren't automatically moving to do as he wanted.

'I don't have to do what he says, either,' Cassie told Jared. It had been a secret, but now her defiance seemed to also transfer to Jared. *'Nate told me to just act like I had to, in order to keep your father happy.'*

'It's probably best if I do the same,' he added, still unsure why he didn't have to follow his alpha's command.

Jared gently turned Cassie around so that she faced the girl in the middle of the monsters. Several men in the circle had already transformed. The young girl couldn't have been much older than Cassie, maybe a couple years at the most. She stared across the space to Cassie. Jared kept his arms around her waist, and she gripped him tight. She knew what they planned and really didn't want to see it. She didn't know the girl, but the young witch could have been anyone Cassie had grown up with.

"Paul, I believe you have won the honors of the first drink tonight," Ben called to the man who had brought the girl into the circle.

The curly-haired man stepped forward. Maybe in his twenties, Cassie had no idea who he was either, but he looked familiar. She didn't know the wendigo or the skinwalkers well for the most part, and she had never been allowed to leave town on her own to meet anyone else. Now she wanted to know more. Was he familiar because he used to be a skinwalker?

'Yes. He was kicked out by the clan three years ago. He's from a different town, but he has a couple cousins here. We took him in when he had nowhere else to go,' Jared explained in response to Cassie's mental questions.

"I wish to take her as my mate," Paul told Ben.

Ben shrugged. "I know my son demonstrated for you all something that you thought was impossible, but just so you know, it doesn't always work that way. The bond is a curious thing. Some are meant to be, and others are not. If you want to take that chance, so be it, but if the bond doesn't take, you will be the one to take her life."

Paul looked up at Ben. The alpha was serious, and Cassie could feel his eagerness at the witch dying. Ben didn't think the bond would work at all.

Pushing Jared's hands down, Cassie walked into the circle. Jared reached for her to stop her, but Ben halted him.

"Let her go. She needs to know this is how it works. The witches raised her to think the world a kind and beautiful place. It doesn't work that way in any clan. She needs to understand that and come to the real world. She bonded to you, and is one of us now. Let her go."

Cassie walked up to the girl. It seemed like the girl wanted to talk but couldn't do so. She stared with her haunted gray eyes at Cassie. The girl's dress was perfect without even a wrinkle, even though she already had been fed upon several times. Bite marks lined her arms and neck. Cassie wanted to feel her own neck but knew that her bond healed everything instantly.

Reaching up, she placed her hands on the cheeks of the girl. She wanted to see her past and her future. Cassie needed to understand why this girl was there and why Cassie had to see her die. Ben was completely right. Cassie had been raised and trained by the witches to believe Mother Earth was kind and gentle. She had been taught that if you treated the world with kindness, you would receive kindness in return. Cassie had never really received kindness from her peers, but she never worried about being taken into the woods to be eaten by monsters.

"Why did you leave your clan?" Cassie asked. Images flowed to Cassie.

The girl stood in front of a priestess for a coven. Two other girls about the same age stood beside her. Next to the coven priestess was a young man, not as young as the teenage girls, but at least not in his thirties yet as the two previous men had been. The man came forward and sniffed each girl, running his hands over the front of him as he looked like he was assessing each. He walked back to the priestess.

'I'll take the middle one,' he told her.

The other two girls on each side of her bowed and hurried out of the room. The girl the wendigoes had found was left alone with the priestess and the young man.

'You will be bonded at tomorrow night's ceremony,' the priestess told the girl. She nodded and bowed before leaving.

Outside the door to the room, the girl finally began to cry. She didn't like the guy and surely didn't want to spend her life with him. She knew him from growing up in town even though they were far enough in age to have never gone to school together. There were too many reasons she

177

couldn't even list them all. What was she supposed to do? The priestess' word was law. The girl didn't have a choice.

The images flashed forward to the woods. The girl was running. She made her choice. She'd rather be free and alone than be with that man. Her family, the coven, her life, it was all done. She would have to start over. That was it.

Cassie pulled out of her thoughts.

"You wanted to be free," Cassie whispered. The girl's eyes grew wide, like Cassie knew a deep, dark secret.

Sighing, Cassie closed her eyes. Freedom was a myth. No one was ever truly free, or if they were, Cassie had yet to meet them. Would death make the girl free?

Cassie looked back into her eyes. New images flashed.

The girl was sitting outside a barn, a familiar red barn that seemed to be a staple at each of the houses the wendigo had. She was watching two little boys run around outside as she rocked a baby in her arms. Soon enough a young man came from the woods. His smile made her heart beat like crazy even after all the years together. The girl was happy. And her heart was free.

Cassie pulled back, a bit disorientated. She was used to seeing the past, but she was sure it was the future she just saw. Cassie looked at the girl who didn't seem to notice anything new. She was still terrified. Turning, Cassie searched the circle of men. The blond she had seen in the future was standing off to the east.

"He's your mate," Cassie stated, pointing at the young man. He seemed shocked by what Cassie was saying as much as the girl had.

Ben laughed behind Cassie. "This is a good show," he commented. "Sure, let's go with that one. Paul, sorry, my son's mate would like Marc to have the first meal tonight. You will lead us in the next ceremony."

Paul bowed to Ben before backing up. Cassie could feel the relief pour off him. He didn't want to kill the girl at all.

Marc walked forward to the girl and Cassie. The girl

stared at Marc with as much horror as she had Paul. Cassie stopped the girl from looking at him by turning to face her.

'He's your mate, but the choice is yours. You either choose him and find the future I know you should have, or you choose to reject him and death will follow. He's a good man and will kill you swiftly if you choose death. It may not be what you wanted from your life, but you still get to choose.' Cassie mentally projected to the girl. She was certain the girl had heard, since her face changed from horror to curiosity.

Cassie walked back to Jared, and his arms snaked back around her middle to hold her in place, in case she wanted to interrupt what was to come.

The girl stared up to the wendigo in front of her. After he bit down on his wrist, he held it out for her. She didn't hesitate as she opened her mouth and drank the blood he was offering. She closed her eyes when he transformed and quickly moved to bite down on her neck. Just as Jared had acted, Marc moved back and his earlier wendigo features faded away; he became a deep gray form of a human with a dog-like face.

The crowd around the two stared in stunned silence. Marc reached down and broke the chains holding the girl in place before scooping her into his arms.

"Guess you're going to get your couple dozen wendigo pups now, Father," Jared commented, breaking the silence. The men were still quietly watching the girl as she was carried away. He didn't even stop at the edge of the circle as he kept walking into the woods with her.

Ben glanced down at Cassie in Jared's arms. He was completely curious about her now.

"I've never trusted the coven," Cassie told Ben. "They might have preached in all things good, but I wasn't raised as one of them. I don't believe all they say, but I do believe in fate. That girl was meant to find the wendigo, as her destined mate was always here."

The men in the circle all stared at her.

"How did you know she should be with Marc?" Ryder asked, finally speaking from his father's other side. Ben was still silent, and Cassie didn't know if that was a good or bad thing.

"I remembered my past, and I know who I am now," Cassie answered.

"She was supposed to be the next seer for the whole coven," Jared explained as all the men hung on every word being spoken. Ryder already knew that much, but now that Cassie knew, it made all the difference.

Ben smiled like everything clicked into place. "Son, you have brought us the seer as your mate. This calls for a celebration." There was actual joy behind the evilness that came off Ben. "Paul, Mitch, and Neil, go get us something to eat from the caves. We all need a bit of blood to make this a feast. My son and beta has brought us victory over the skinwalkers. That's reason enough for us to get drunk on witch blood tonight. Make sure you bring enough for everyone."

Three men left the circle and hurried away. Cassie leaned back against Jared. They were going to feed upon more witches since she saved the last. Ben wasn't about to give up his lust for blood.

Cassie was tired from seeing into the future. This was the first time she had been able to do so since she was a kid, and it felt odd, but right at the same time. It was like since Jared unblocked her memories, there was much more she could do that she never knew was possible. The coven had taken all of that away from her.

"I'm taking her back home," Jared told his father as he scooped Cassie into his arms.

Ben opened his eyes in shock at his son's directness.

"She's weak from using her sight. If I keep her out here much longer, she's going to pass out from exhaustion. I can feel her pulling on my energy to just keep going," Jared explained. Cassie hadn't known she was doing that.

Ben nodded and waved his hand like he was dismissing them. "Your loss. Now that you know how good witch blood tastes, maybe you'll give up that hospital crap you keep in your fridge."

Jared only nodded at his father. He had no intention of feeding off anyone, especially not the witches they had kidnapped.

'Kidnapped?' Cassie asked, suddenly finding a speck of reserved energy. Nate and John were freeing the kidnapped witches tonight. The three wendigo were going there, too.

Ben's head snapped up as he instantly changed into his wendigo form. Cassie was surprised at how fast he changed, but even more surprised to see that Ben actually wasn't any bigger than Jared was in his form.

Cassie felt a snap, like she had been smacked with a rubber band. Directing her gaze at Jared, she saw him staring in the direction his father was now storming away. She hadn't felt it directly, but through the bond with Jared.

'What's going on?' Cassie asked.

'Neil is dead. Someone just killed him,' Jared explained, picturing one of the men who had just walked away to get the witches.

CHAPTER 11

Jared didn't waste any time; he changed instantly into his new wendigo form. Scooping Cassie into his arms, he ran a little bit from the outcrop of stones and into the woods. He jumped into the trees with her in his arms, and gently set her down once they were in the clear. Taking off his coat, which he had picked up on the way, he wrapped it around her shoulders. There was very little commotion below, yet he was leaving her. Jared turned to go, but Cassie refused to let go of his arm.

'What's going on? What was that I felt?' Cassie asked silently. She could feel the wendigo not too far away, but where they were it was eerily quiet.

'Someone attacked Neil,' Jared explained. *'The alpha is linked to the clan, and as the beta, so am I. When someone dies, I feel it.'*

'The witches?' She was hopeful they were the ones breaking free.

'Doubtful. Their magic had been drained, and they were locked away,' Jared replied. Cassie realized that by worrying, Jared might have searched her mind, but she never thought to search his. He was the beta. He knew where the witches were. *'They couldn't get out, otherwise they would have already left.'*

The silence of the night was shattered. Cassie heard a roar where she sat in the tree. There was definitely a big cat below in the direction of the wendigo. More animal noises sounded before Jared moved to leave again.

'You can't leave me here,' Cassie complained. Animals

meant more than likely Nate and her uncle, and anyone else they could find.

'Cas, I have to. Many of those men below aren't strong enough to protect themselves. I have to go down there and help,' Jared explained, looking through the trees with his night vision.

She didn't want Jared to go risk his life for a bunch of men who planned to feed off and drain innocent witches. *'But—'*

Kneeling beside Cassie, he took her face in his hands. *'There are bad men in every group just like there are bad witches. Many of them are as far from innocent as you can get. But you had to have seen it with the girl. There are good ones here, too. There are ones who refuse to kill a witch to grow in power. There are ones that are here because of the coven and clan kicking them out. There are good men down there. I need to go protect them,'* Jared explained. *'They don't stand a chance against your uncle or Nate in their pledge forms. They need me.'*

Cassie understood. The fellow she had just partnered with the young witch was a good man. There was no evil in his head like Ben. Jared was right, even if she didn't want to admit it, and she was positive the skinwalkers weren't going to see the difference. They had been raised to view the wendigo as all bad and the skinwalkers all good, with nothing in between.

"Stay safe," Cassie whispered, knowing she had to let him go.

Jared quickly kissed her before disappearing instantly down below. Cassie squinted into the darkness but could see nothing. She heard it, though. The long scraping of wendigo nails on the rocks as they all transformed to meet the skinwalkers coming for them. Cassie grasped the tree when she heard the roar of a bear. She had seen bears at the zoo before and had heard them roar, but it was nothing like what she heard now. It was as if the whole ground was shaking from his roar. Cassie had no doubts to who that was. Uncle John was down there, fighting the same battle as Jared. He was keeping the younger skinwalkers safe. John wasn't a killer; he was a protector. Cassie's heart picked up speed. She hated being locked away from it all. Another roar reverberated through the woods. Nate had to be there, too.

Grasping the tree, she peered through the leaves to see if there was a way down. Her family, her friends, and Jared were all there below. Everyone she cared about was about to fight. Unfortunately, there wasn't a good foothold to get down with. She would have to jump, and she was afraid it would be a bad idea. If she got hurt, so did Jared, and she didn't need to make him vulnerable.

Cassie wanted to know what was going on as the air stilled around her. They were on the verge of something, and she was sitting in a tree in the dark. She concentrated on Jared and the bond between them. It only took a little feeling to get into his head. It was like watching a movie as it played in real time. She could see what he was seeing and that made her feel a bit better, until she realized what he was looking at. A line of carnivore animals made a half moon around the outcropping of stones where they had just been standing. At the middle of the pack of animals were two tigers and a bear. Cassie immediately recognized them, and her stomach dropped. Other bears and even a couple more tigers made up the front line, but the two she was worried about were obvious to her. Nate stood beside what had to be his father. Their markings were identical, except his father was white and black while Nate was orange and black.

'Don't hurt them,' Cassie begged Jared.

'I don't want to hurt anyone, but I will defend the wendigo. I can't let innocent people get caught in the middle.' Jared was as much in the middle as an innocent person. He was as far from his father's ways as one could get.

That wasn't a yes or no, but Cassie figured she wasn't

getting any better response from him. She could already feel the conflicted feelings inside of him. He didn't want to fight anyone, but he was backed into a corner as much as the skinwalkers had been since their witches had been taken away.

Uncle John stood up on his hind legs, and in doing so had to be over eight feet tall. He roared, and the animals around him responded. Cassie couldn't shake the images of the future she had once seen. John was always supposed to be alpha while Mikel raised Nate. Cassie had to wonder what it would have been like then. She knew the wendigo and skinwalkers were sworn enemies, but would it still be the same? John was a much fairer person, and even in his bear form was a more reasonable than Mikel.

Bear John sat back down on all fours, which seemed to be the signal to everyone because they rushed forward. Not to be outdone, Ben raised his arm and signaled for the wendigo to meet them in the middle.

Jared didn't watch his father as he followed everyone into the fight. Cassie could hear from her tree when the night creatures hit each other head on. She pulled out of Jared's mind momentarily to look with her own eyes into the night. Her friends were below fighting, and there was nothing she could do.

Focusing, Cassie moved back to Jared's mind. He was in the middle of the mess of creatures as they swung, cut, bit, and did so much more to each other. Blood was everywhere, and his senses were picking up on the mixture of wendigo and skinwalker. When he felt another wendigo get chopped down, he would move to save them. Cassie's heart beat wildly while Jared moved through the crowd, keeping his own men safe and never outright attacking the skinwalkers. Cassie didn't know if it was for her sake or if that was just his way—any move on a skinwalker was non-lethal.

Jared ducked as another animal came charging toward him. His new power gave him even better reflexes than normal. Cassie was dizzy by how fast he could move. The skinwalker didn't stand a chance, yet again, Jared didn't kill him when he could. Jared turned to see his father scream in rage. He wasn't as kind and bodies were piling up by his feet. Jared knew that his father was creating a target of himself, but he didn't care. He relished in the fight and his hatred of the skinwalkers, the hatred that had kicked him out of the clan almost a decade ago poured from him, fueling his rage further.

Quickly, Jared searched for the next person to help. He didn't bother to help the group that was attacking the bear John. They were all the same as his father—vengeful for blood. None of the mess was John's fault. Jared respected the man who'd raised Cassie. He understood that he was just like Jared. He was protecting his own. Six wendigo in their pledge forms took turns attacking him, but John was fine. Jared moved on.

Several skinwalkers moved to attack his father. Jared had to step in. It was his job to support his dad, no matter how crazy he was. As Jared approached, his pathway was cut off. A large white tiger stood in his way. Mikel nipped at Jared, and he backed away from the alpha, quick enough to keep his arm but not quick enough to go help his father.

Jared glanced at his father again, and the older alpha laughed as four skinwalkers attacked at once. Jared jumped as Mikel moved in and swiped his tiger paws at Jared's legs. He had very little memory of Mikel beyond the fatherly figure he was to Nate, but his father had told him enough stories for Jared to know Mikel was cut from the same cloth as his own father. Mikel attacked again, and Jared had to quickly move. Ben finally noticed Jared.

"Is that how we play now?" Ben asked, throwing down the fourth skinwalker he was toying with. Cassie couldn't tell if they were all dead or just hurt.

Ben jumped over the pile of animals around him and stalked into the fight of people. As he passed skinwalker and wendigo fighting, he didn't stop to help anyone. He was on a direct march to the tiger that was fending off his own horde of attackers. Tipping his head back, Ben screeched into the night. The wendigo who had been attacking Nate backed away, leaving Nate facing Ben.

She pulled out of Jared's mind. It was too much. She could feel the thirst for vengeance in Ben. He was out for blood, and Nate was his target. Cassie wasn't bonded to Nate, and his life ending wouldn't end hers unless the bond came back. But she didn't want him hurt, let alone dead.

Cassie looked around. She didn't have anything with her and had yet to learn how to fight with magic. She was useless, and now her family was out there fighting and possibly dying if Ben got to them.

She was far enough away from the fighting that she was able to hear the low growl beneath her. Glancing down, she dreaded which skinwalker had found her. She wasn't bonded to Nate and didn't know what that meant for her now. Would they be her enemy? The witches had made it clear Nate was going to have to kill her if she joined the wrong side. The bond with him wasn't back yet. She was still technically the enemy.

The large mountain lion looked up the tree at her before climbing up. Backing away on the branch, she tried not to freak out. Jared had tucked her away, and he needed to concentrate on what he was doing. She calmed her heartbeat and looked at the animal that was now staring at her. Cassie couldn't distract Jared. He was facing off with Mikel.

The golden-colored mountain lion stared at Cassie. It made no move to come and get her, just stared. Cassie stared back, and then it hit her. It was very well possible that she was looking at her best friend.

"Whitney?" Cassie whispered.

The mountain lion gave a sort of smile and nodded her large cat head.

Knowing the large cat was Whitney calmed Cassie a bit

more. Her friend was the one person the alpha didn't order around. Even if Cassie was the enemy now, she was confident Whitney wouldn't hurt her. Cassie crawled forward on the branch back to the trunk of the tree. Whitney stared at Cassie to open the channel between them.

Cassie could already see the first bit of the battle.

Mikel was busy fighting with Jared, while Jared was evading the old alpha, and Ben had already made it to Nate. He had clipped off the tip of Nate's tail with his razor-sharp claws, but hadn't been able to touch him a second time.

"What can I do, Whit? I don't have the power to fight them. I'm just one witch," Cassie complained.

Whitney continued to stare. Cassie felt it better this time. The future was coming to her.

Jared was keeping up with Mikel and not touching the old alpha nor getting a single scratch on himself. Mikel slowly was wearing down, yet Jared still wouldn't go in for the kill. He didn't even make a single offensive move on the older alpha.

Nate wasn't fairing as well. He already had two cuts running the length of his cat body. Ben had tried to gut him the last time Nate moved in to attack him. Ben was playing cat and mouse with Nate, except Nate didn't happen to be the cat in the equation. Where Mikel and Jared were playing it safe, Ben and Nate were going all out. Ben might have been as cut up as Nate was, but Cassie could see it. Nate didn't have the strength to keep up with him. Without his bond to her, Nate wasn't the alpha he was always meant to become. He needed a bonded witch to do that. Cassie cringed when Ben moved again, slicing through Nate's back left leg. The beautiful tiger fell to the ground.

Cassie pulled out of the future. It was one she didn't want to see. One she had to prevent.

"Can you take me to them?" she asked her cat friend. She was dizzy from looking into the future, but that didn't stop anything. Whitney nodded.

Cassie climbed on the back of her friend who was twice the size of a normal cougar. Cat Whitney easily leapt from the tree without causing either girl a broken bone. She held on as Whitney moved right into the fight of everyone. Whitney stopped an equal distance from both guys. Animals and monsters were fighting all around them, and not even noticing them as they stood.

She didn't know what to do, but when all else failed, her aunt had always told her to call on old Mother Earth. Cassie knelt in the ground, digging a quick hold in the dirt. Pulling out the pocket knife she had gotten from Jared, she sliced into her hand and dropped her blood into the ground.

"Mother, please hear my prayer. Give me the strength to stop this," Cassie whispered a prayer before placing her hands on the ground where her blood had just been soaked up. She wasn't sure what to do, but decided to just follow her instincts.

"Everyone, stop! Freeze," Cassie commanded, knowing more than one life depended on her stopping everything.

At her command, everyone—including the alphas—stopped in their tracks. It appeared they had been frozen in place. Cassie even imagined she could see ice on the feet of the person nearest her. As she stood, she could tell no one was moving except her. It was time for her to take back control of her life, starting with the fighting around her.

Cassie walked between a wendigo fighting with a wolf, making sure not to touch or come between them. As she got near Nate, Ben's eyes followed her though he couldn't move his body. He again was studying her, but Cassie didn't care. She wasn't about to let him kill Nate.

Reaching forward, Cassie touched Nate. He unfroze at the same time as she felt the bond snap back into place. She could feel him in her head again. Their bond was back, and luckily his tail was healed.

'Did they do anything to you?' Nate asked across the bond. He had felt it bind into place.

'No, I'm fine.'

Turning, Cassie walked back through the mess of people over to Jared. She touched him, and the frozen spell on him was instantly gone. He looked at Nate and gave him a frown.

'The bond is back,' she told Jared.

Jared nodded as Cassie moved once again. This time, she went to the north end of the stone outcrop. No one seemed to notice they had been fighting in the ritual spot of the wendigo, or if they did, no one seemed to care. She kind of thought it was the latter.

Cassie stood on the north stone and faced the night humans that had been fighting. Slowly they were back to moving, yet no one charged an inch to fight again. Even Nate and Jared's fathers, the alphas, waited to assess the situation.

"I didn't create this mess, but I'm sick of it," Cassie began as she looked at all the faces, monsters and animals alike. "I can't understand why everyone hates each other, but I'm missing something here. Where is the coven in all this?"

Not a single witch was on the fighting ground. In fact, Cassie could tell through the bond with Nate that the coven had fled back to the city already while the skinwalkers came in to fight. Even Maria was gone, but Cassie had a feeling that it had more to do with John sending her away than anything. Cassie was the only day human left standing in the middle of the bloodbath the night humans created together.

Ben smiled smugly at tiger Mikel.

"And I understand the fighting to take back the coven since everyone is stuck in their animal forms," Cassie added. Ben's smile faded. "But what I don't understand is why all the fighting to begin with?"

Cassie felt the jumble of thoughts push from both sides. Each person there was fighting for their own reasons, but no one seemed to agree on what those reasons were. Even in each clan. Skinwalkers had several ideas while wendigo all disagreed on their reasons.

"Stop," Cassie ordered, her head spinning from all the thoughts running through it. It was worse than before. The voices of everyone around her were louder for some reason.

Everyone stopped thinking and stared at her.

'I could get used to this,' Cassie told Nate and Jared.

"You know what," Cassie addressed the crowd, "I'm sick of all the reasons and all the lies. I found out once I was with the wendigo that my whole childhood had been changed by the coven. I have just as many reasons to hate them as the wendigo, but I don't. Someone taught me to look beyond the few bad people in a group. The coven didn't change my memories and my fate. Certain people did. I won't blame the coven, and no one here should blame a whole side of people either."

Ben began to walk forward.

"What the coven did is unforgivable, but the fact that Mikel let them is why I fight here," he explained, slowly moving closer, but toward Nate in general. "I deserve my vengeance."

Ben wasn't moving fast, but was threatening enough. Cassie could tell exactly what he was planning, and she dropped to her knees to pull power from the ground again to freeze him in his place. Everyone around her just stared. Ben was the alpha, and she was stopping him. Then what did that make her?

"I'm sorry for stopping you like this in front of everyone, but I need to before you make a mistake," Cassie told Ben, hoping to soothe him. His anger was growing every minute he couldn't move. He had never been anywhere but at the top of the food chain before.

"If you kill Nate, you will kill Jared also because we are all three bonded together."

"Impossible," Ben spat out. His anger was boiling, but so was his curiosity. He denied her based on logic, yet he was smart enough to keep an open mind.

"I was forced to bond to Nate a week ago when your own son and my cousin took Nate. They wanted my protection spell and forced me to cast it on him first. In the process, he took some of my blood. This would have been fine if Ryder hadn't attacked me the day before and Nate used his blood to heal me. We bonded instantly because of what Ryder and Jack both did," Cassie explained.

"Still impossible. Once bonded you can't take another," Ben stated, obviously not believing her story.

"And I've heard you can't have two mates, but that doesn't seem to be the case either," Cassie pointed out. She had him there; even he couldn't explain it.

"When you said Jared would have to kill me if he couldn't bond to me, I temporarily broke the bond with Nate, so I could bind with Jared. I had no clue what would happen after that, but it seems it's possible to have two people bonded to one." Cassie shrugged. That was as much as she could explain it because she really had no clue beyond that.

"I still don't believe you," Ben said, his fingers beginning to wiggle.

Cassie didn't have much more time of his being frozen. Her words weren't convincing him, and he would believe Jared even less. He had seen Jared fighting and was already mad at him for not killing anyone. Cassie clenched her hands. Alphas could be impossible to deal with. Her hand gripped the pocket knife she was still holding.

"Fine. I'll prove it," Cassie added.

'I need you in human form for this,' Cassie told Nate. She slipped off Jared's coat she was wearing as Nate transformed beside her. Keeping her eyes closed, she handed him the coat.

Nate chuckled. He was completely fine with being nude around all the men and animals, but he wrapped the coat around his waist anyway for Cassie. She reopened her eyes when she knew he was covered ... well, the front of him was covered.

Turning to Nate, she took his hands and held them out parallel to the ground. "Keep them there," Cassie instructed.

He held them in place as asked.

"Now you," Cassie said, turning to Jared.

Ben was almost free, but he wasn't moving toward them again. He was watching Cassie with the same analyzing look he had many times already since she had met him.

Taking the knife, Cassie held it above Jared's left hand. Her hands shook at the thought of cutting him. Jared smiled as he placed his hand over hers and pressed down. They had just been fighting for their lives, so a thin cut that would barely bleed on the top of his hand was nothing in comparison.

Cassie felt the skin on her hand break open. She turned to Nate. He was now sporting the same cut across his left hand. Ben looked shocked, but Cassie wasn't done yet. She needed both Ben and Mikel to see that they couldn't touch each other's children. It was the only way Nate and Jared would both stay safe.

She held the knife over Nate's right hand. He didn't even wait for her to hesitate as he pressed the knife down. The skin broke open on her other hand, and followed on Jared.

Cassie looked up at Ben finally. He saw the mark on his own son and was astonished, even if he hid it well. The frozen spell wore off, and he could move freely, but he made no more movements toward Nate.

"We are in a stalemate," Cassie told the two alphas. "It's best we all learn to get along. I have no idea what that means, but it has been a long few weeks, and I want some sleep. Everyone go home. We will have to talk this over some other time." Cassie yawned. Seeing into the future was really exhausting.

Ben finally agreed with Cassie. Tilting his head back, he gave a few roars into the sky. The wendigo vanished from their spots beside whoever they were fighting. Nate handed

Cassie the coat and shifted back into his tiger form. Ben stood on the west side of the circle, staring across at Mikel.

Mikel roared, and most of the skinwalkers disappeared into the night also. A big, brown-colored bear waited at the edge of the woods.

'Time to go home,' tiger Nate told Cassie in her head. *'My mother should be there waiting for us.'*

Cassie glanced down at him. They were once again bonded, and he was telling her what to do. Typical Nate.

"Cassie?" Jared asked, holding out his hand for her.

Cassie smiled at him. He wasn't bossy like Nate, but she didn't plan to go back to his place either. There was only one place she really wanted to go.

"Sorry, guys. I got somewhere to be." Cassie perched on her toes and pulled Jared down to give him a kiss on his cheek before she patted Nate on his big, furry head.

Cassie didn't even stop to look at their shocked faces. Well, she knew Jared wasn't shocked. He was actually grinning at her as she ran away. Nate was busy sulking already. Cassie ran to the edge of the woods to the waiting bear.

"Can we finally go home now, Uncle John?"

The bear roared his response.

"Good. Because I really miss my bed, and I think I might be able to sleep all winter with you this year."

Bear John dropped low to the ground, offering her a ride just like she had seen Maria doing. Laughing, Cassie climbed on all the fur. If it wasn't for the fur, she could pretend she was little again, getting a piggyback ride from her uncle who thought the world of her. Cassie smiled as she snuggled into his fur. A furry uncle was fun, too. But even better was knowing that he never tossed her aside. He had always loved her and taken care of her. Even as all the memories mixed together, Cassie was happy to be able to say she had a home to go back to.

Cassie turned back to see Nate and Jared still standing

where she left them. She waved to them as John began to run.

'We'll talk about this in the morning,' Nate told Cassie.

'Goodnight, Cas. Tell Maria I say hi,' Jared added to Cassie's mind.

Cassie smiled into John's fur. She had her two best friends back. She might not want to be bonded to anyone, and seemed to be gaining mates by the week, but she was still happy. When she had sliced Nate's hand, she felt it. He had his memories back now, too. That wasn't going to change things instantly, but it was a start. Being bonded to both of them was a great beginning on the road to finding a solution between the wendigo and the skinwalkers. And she was ready to go home and get some sleep. It might have taken a little work, but things were starting to seem a little more normal.

ACKNOWLEDGEMENTS

To you, the reader. <u>Thank you</u> for taking the time to read this story and go on the journey with me. If you liked it, please leave a review on your favorite online bookseller (or all of them!) and connect with me social media. The greatest help you can do to keep a writer going is to support them by spreading the word about their books.

Also I would like to thank my editors and cover designers. A good editor is essential to getting the story correct (and in my case- two editors). Thank you so much, Kathie at Kat's Eye Editing and Melissa at There for You Editing. It would not be the same book without them. Also a thanks to my proofer Ashton Brammer for going over the novel with a fine tooth comb to catch little errors that bug people. A thank-you to my *AMAZING* cover artist Jessica for such a pretty cover. An awesome cover helps get people interested. I greatly appreciate all those that can do what I cannot, like editors and cover designers. I'm thankful I was able to find wonderful professionals to work with on this book.

I'd also like to thank my hubby for continuing to push me further down the writing road. He gives me time when I need it to work on my stories. He encourages me to keep going each and every day on this adventure. And he does all the behind-the-scenes effort to make this work (have you seen my trailers- he is awesome!). This would be so much harder without his help. So thank you, B. for pushing me off the deep end (or the cliff as I see it sometimes). And a great big thanks to my little munchkins who keep me going from before the sun comes up 'til long after it sets. Love you AK, KB, and EM.

<u>Thank you so much for taking the time to read my novel!!</u>

ABOUT B. KRISTIN MCMICHAEL

Originally from Wisconsin, B. Kristin currently resides in Ohio with her husband, three small children, and three cats. A former cell biologist, she now does the mom thing of chasing kids, baking cookies, and playing outside while writing full time. She is a fan of all YA/NA fantasy and science fiction. Find her at www.bkristinmcmichael.com and Twitter, Facebook, Instagram, and Goodreads under B. Kristin McMichael.

OTHER BOOKS BY
B KRISTIN McMICHAEL

- To Stand Beside Her

Chalcedony Chronicles
- Carnelian
- Chrysoprase
- Aventurine
- Chrysocolla

The Night Human World series:

The Blue Eyes Trilogy (series 1)
- The Legend of the Blue Eyes
- Becoming a Legend
- Winning the Legend

The Day Human Trilogy (series 2)
- The Day Human Prince
- The Day Human King
- The Day Human Way

The Skinwalkers Witchling Trilogy (series 3)
- The Witchling's Apprentice
- The Wendigo Witchling
- The Witchling Seer (coming soon)

www.ingramcontent.com/pod-product-compliance
Lightning Source LLC
Chambersburg PA
CBHW060933180626
46817CB00004B/1514

* 9 7 8 1 9 4 1 7 4 5 8 3 0 *